SWITCHING
THE ODDS

Stonewall Inn Mysteries
Michael Denneny, General Editor

DEATH TAKES THE STAGE
by Donald Ward

SHERLOCK HOLMES AND THE MYSTERIOUS FRIEND OF OSCAR WILD
by Russell A. Brown

A SIMPLE SUBURBAN MURDER
by Mark Richard Zubro

A BODY TO DYE FOR
by Grant Michaels

WHY ISN'T BECKY TWITCHELL DEAD?
by Mark Richard Zubro

THE ONLY GOOD PRIEST
by Mark Richard Zubro

SORRY NOW?
by Mark Richard Zubro

THIRD MAN OUT
by Richard Stevenson

LOVE YOU TO DEATH
by Grant Michaels

THE NIGHT G.A.A. DIED
by Jack Ricardo

SWITCHING THE ODDS
by Phyllis Knight

SWITCHING THE ODDS

PHYLLIS KNIGHT

ST. MARTIN'S PRESS
NEW YORK

SWITCHING THE ODDS: A LIL RITCHIE MYSTERY. Copyright © 1992 by Phyllis Knight. All rights reserved. Printed in the United States of America. No part of this book may be used or reproduced in any manner whatsoever without written permission except in the case of brief quotations embodied in critical articles or reviews. For information, address St. Martin's Press, 175 Fifth Avenue, New York, N.Y. 10010.

Design by Dawn Niles

Library of Congress Cataloging-in-Publication Data

Knight, Phyllis.
    Switching the odds: a Lil Ritchie mystery / Phyllis Knight.
        p. cm.
    ISBN 0-312-07865-X (hc)
    ISBN 0-312-09400-0 (pbk.)
    I. Title.
    PS3561.N488S93   1992
    813'.54—dc20

                                                                92-3013
                                                                CIP

First Edition: June 1992

10 9 8 7 6 5 4 3 2 1

To Yolande, who invited the San Francisco rocker, but who never faltered when a country girl, a beat poet, and a beastie accompanied her to the door.

ACKNOWLEDGMENTS

To the members of my Cabinet: John Willie and Juanita, Laila Begum, Ann Bingham, Carol Trimble, and Mary McCormick, thanks so much for your generosity and knowledge.

To Chica Teutsch, John Penkalski, Berta Goodman, Brecon Oldham, Robin Ito, and my buddies at the Ellsworth Public Library, my heartfelt thanks.

Special gratitude goes to Owen Raynor, Thelma Guild, and Shirley Clements, three teachers who made a difference, and to my mother, Althea Highlander, who never once tried to censor what her young daughter read, or threw away a single scrap of paper with her writing on it.

To my big sister, Nancy, my first singing partner, thanks for taking me as I am, and for showing me what courage and bravery are all about.

To my family in Virginia, and the infamous Charlottesville Girls, thanks, guys, for the continuity you bring to my life. As you well know, I need it!

Much appreciation also to my agent, Norman Laurila, for his quiet competence and support, to Michael Denneny, my editor, for adding to the vision, and to Keith Kahla, for looking after the details.

Neale, wherever you are, I did it. Thanks for the challenge, your last gift.

All my relations. All my relations. All my relations.

"Things are not what they seem, nor are they otherwise."
—Lankavatara Sutra

"Escape is so simple
In a world where sunsets can be raced.
But distance only loses the knife
the pattern of its scar
can always be traced."
—Michael Timmins, "Escape Is So Simple"
[The Cowboy Junkies]

SWITCHING
THE ODDS

ONE

I'd been spending the morning looking out of my office window, watching the snow come down in clean white sheets. The filth that had accumulated on top of the snowbanks this long winter had finally been covered over during the last hour, and things now looked the way they do on the postcards that say "Typical New England Winter Scene." I was giving it another half-day at best.

By this first day of March we'd already had more snow than this part of the state had seen in fifty years. The mud season that was certain to follow in a month or so reminded me of the local joke about the weather: "nine months of winter followed by three months of damned poor sledding." I'm convinced that gallows humor started in the North Country.

This was only my second winter here, and half of me was settling in but the other half couldn't wait to escape. To me, this was a familiar war. It had already been fought and lost in a half-dozen of some of the more interesting places in the country, California, Texas, and several spots in northern New Mexico among them. Most places take a while to grow on you, and some never do—until you leave.

But today's mail would already be sitting in my box at the bottom of the stairs and I was looking forward to an early lunch before tackling the backlog of paperwork that was staring me in the face.

I closed my eyes for the briefest of moments, enjoying a fantasy of spring, somewhere far away, where flowers bloomed and the air smelled sweet. I was jerked out of my reverie by the sounds of a door opening and closing in the hallway, followed by voices that carried through the thin walls. Molly Byrne was sending a client on his way.

I smiled to myself. Molly and I had known each other so long we were as comfortable as a beer and a shot. It had been her long letters full of praise for the ocean and the people of Maine that had turned a particular tide for me; I'd thrown my few decent possessions into a Ryder truck and headed north nearly two years before, driving until the intensity of the north woods took over the landscape both inside and outside my head. Molly, a lawyer with a conscience, had been my ace in the hole—she'd given all her investigation work to me, and had urged a couple of colleagues to do the same, and somehow I'd found myself making a living, more or less, in Down East Maine. Sometimes you just never know.

Molly poked her head through my doorway. "You want to have lunch, Lil? It's a little early, but you don't seem to be exactly overwhelmed with work."

It was the best offer I'd had all day. I raised an eyebrow in a way that always made her laugh. "Where? Want to go to Pat's?"

Pat's Diner was our favorite, and we seldom went anywhere else, barring a sudden craving for Chinese.

"Yeah." She glanced at her watch. "Give me five minutes and we can walk down together, maybe even get a booth this early. I've just got to turn my computer off and make a quick call."

Lunch held no surprises, which was why we liked to go to Pat's. When I got back to the office the phone was ringing. A crisp and formal female voice said, "Is this the Lillian Ritchie Detective Agency?"

I said that it was. "Detective Agency" has that prosperous sound I like. I figured that by the time clients found out I worked alone they would already be too committed to switch to a larger agency. My mother has lain awake many a night worrying about this side of my nature.

"One moment, please. Mr. Cooper wishes to speak to you."

This was a deep male voice. "Miss Ritchie, my name is James Cooper and I'm calling from Richmond, Virginia. You've been recommended to me for a personal matter that needs some looking into."

Ah, Virginia. That explained the "Miss" Ritchie and the rich, slow delivery. If my native Virginia was Southern, Richmond was just a little more so. My friend Richard always says about Richmond: "We're a little behind the times, but we're relaxed."

Relaxed, maybe. But foolish too? Why would anyone call over eight hundred miles for a private dick?

"Mr. Cooper, you need a detective in eastern Maine though you live in the South. That makes me think this must be a long story. Maybe you'd better start from the top."

"It's my son, Jesse, Miss Ritchie. He goes to a prep school here in Richmond, one of the very finest. He's quite a smart boy, a little unfocused perhaps, but brains, he's got. We generally get in touch every few days, and his mother wanted him to come over for Sunday dinner after church. I went over to pick him up and he was gone."

"Gone? How'd he get away with that?"

"I told you he's a smart boy. On Thursday night he went to the headmaster and told him his grandfather had been taken gravely ill and that the family was going to Virginia Beach right away to look after him. He said his mother had called and was so upset he didn't have all the details. Apparently Jesse put on such a good act that no one suspected a thing."

"And you checked with his grandfather, I suppose?"

There was suddenly enough silence coming from Cooper's end of the line that I could tell he was weighing what he was going to say next. I heard him take a long, deep breath and let it out slowly. When he spoke next there was a weariness in his tone, and something else I couldn't quite name. "My son does not have a grandfather in Virginia Beach. My father-in-law passed away two years ago. He'd always wanted to visit the Holy Land and he was halfway through his vacation there when he had a massive heart attack and went just like that."

"That's one grandfather, Mr. Cooper. That leaves one more," I said softly.

Again there was a silence and a sigh. This time the voice had a hard edge to it. "My son has never seen my father, Miss Ritchie. Perhaps you have, though. I understand he's the town drunk of Tillman, Maine."

I swallowed my surprise like a piece of three-day gum. It hit the pit of my stomach with a murderous little thud and then settled in for the duration. I heard my voice say, "And what would your father's name be?"

"Eugene Cooper. Why? Do you know him?" This voice was as cold as the ice packs along the riverbanks on the outskirts of town.

If "know him" meant "go out to dinner with him," then I was in the clear. But, in a larger sense, I felt I *did* know him. When I first came up here to rent a house, old Eugene had been living in a back room of the place I eventually moved into. The landlord, a kind-natured guy, had felt sorry for the old man and had him caretaking the place until someone moved in. He had been on the wagon for six months and was as shaky as a leaf in the wind. At the time I was all too aware that my moving in meant his having to move out. I'd had two or three conversations with him then—we'd discovered our Virginia connection—and I'd run into him a few times since. No, I didn't *know* him. But a certain sense of him had gotten under my skin and I could feel him like I could feel my own pulse.

"I know who he is, Mr. Cooper, but just how does all this tie in with your son? Has there been some contact?"

"I wish to hell I knew. Jesse started asking me questions about his grandfather last summer, more or less out of the blue. He wanted to know where he'd grown up. Then, a couple of weeks later, we were at a Richmond Braves baseball game and Jesse asked me if my father had taken me to a lot of games when I was a kid. What a laugh! The few times I ever got to go to a game were

4

because my mother worked two shifts in a row in order to take me. And then I was torn between loving her for doing it and not wanting the guys to see me sitting next to my mother in the bleachers."

Cooper broke off abruptly. "Don't ask me why I told you that." He sounded embarrassed.

"So I gather you didn't encourage your son's interest."

"No, I can't say as I did. I thought it was just boyish curiosity and he'd get over it if I didn't say too much. But he kept on with the questions, casual-like. We'd be doing something and Jesse would say, 'Oh, by the way,' like he'd just thought of something right that minute, and he'd come out with the damnedest things. I'm afraid I started cutting him off short, Miss Ritchie. The old son-of-a-bitch never did a thing for me in this life and yet there was my own boy almost more interested in him than in me. You'd better believe that's a hard pill to swallow."

I could, at that. "How old is Jesse, anyway?"

"He'll be seventeen on June the eighth."

Well, he wouldn't have been the first boy or girl to take off after a phantom at that age. I'd almost done it myself, a long time ago.

"I assume you've notified the police already, Mr. Cooper. What do you need me to do for money that the cops won't do for free?"

He cleared his throat. "I've got a gut feeling about this, Miss Ritchie. I'm afraid that Jesse's gone off all half-cocked and hog-wild to look for my old man. Richmond's a pretty big city, you know, but in some ways it's still a small town. I've worked like a dog to get a good name here and I don't want some stupid teenaged brush with the law to—"

He bit the rest of his sentence cleanly in half, but my imagination finished it for him. "You think a private detective would be more—how should I phrase this—discreet?"

"Yes ma'am, I see we understand each other just fine."

His tone had changed again, and now he was just another businessman making a business call in the afternoon of a working day. He was waiting for me to make my move. My heartfelt sympathy had run out a few seconds before.

"I'll see what I can do, Mr. Cooper." I paused for just a moment thinking. "But it'll cost you."

Of that, I was almost certain.

TWO

I hate missing-persons cases. You're either spending your time looking for people who don't want to be found, or finding people who haven't realized they're lost. Half the time you've gotten there too late; the rest of the time you've gotten there before all of the cards have been dealt. You've found your person but you know he won't stay found for long. Missing-persons cases are about heartache taken straight up, no chaser. They're also my specialty. I'm not too sure what that says about me.

I got down to details with James Cooper. I charged him my customary $150 a day plus expenses, with an additional five hundred up front because of the distance involved. That taken care of, I made notes about what he'd told me so far. It wasn't a lot but I'd been known to start with less.

Go figure it. Here's a middle- or upper-middle-class boy in a good, probably expensive school, on his way to the best that life can offer. By now most boys in his shoes would believe it was their due. Around here you see kids his age looking like they were born old, worn down by poverty before they've had a chance to even dream about the good life.

I spent the rest of the afternoon futzing around with my dreaded paperwork, even managing to place a few items into their proper file drawers. Normally, this would give me a large sense of satisfaction, but today some element seemed to be missing. I needed time to think. I looked out of my window at the snow, which was turning to rain, which would turn into sleet before nightfall if I was reading it right. The sky was that pre-dusk gray, at not quite five o'clock. The thought of a cold Dos Equis followed by a hot bath grew more seductive by the minute. I said, "What the hell," to the empty room right before I grabbed for my coat. This mess would have to wait.

I know that people who live alone are only supposed to eat macaroni and cheese right out of the box, but I thought I'd save that for tomorrow night. On my way home I heard a familiar lonesome cry for gumbo and made a small detour to the fish truck that usually parked on top of the hill near the gas stations and fast-food joints leading out of town. A pint of oysters, some fresh crabmeat, a pound of shrimp, and a small piece of hake would be transformed into food fit for the gods, if indeed the gods lived in the bayou country.

My upstairs neighbor, Fred's, truck wasn't in its usual space in the driveway when I got home. I rent the main part of the house, but an earlier owner built a small apartment out of a couple of rooms upstairs, with its own outside entrance around the back. I like living alone, but it's also nice to have a neighbor that close.

Littlefield was sleeping when I opened the back door. By the time I set the fish bag on the kitchen counter, he'd rallied enough for a spontaneous vocal improvisation at my feet. Actually, it was sort of between my feet. When he started rubbing against my legs I knew he'd figured out it was a gumbo night. More than once I'd thought there must be some way to make a buck out of a gumbo-eating cat, but so far he had only cost me money and fish.

I quickly chopped two cups each of onions, green peppers, and celery, and added a handful of chopped garlic to the bowl and set it aside. I poured a cup of good olive oil into my cast-iron pot, and when the oil was smoking hot I added a cup of unbleached white flour. This was the most important moment in Cajun cooking. Here you've got two choices: You can stand there and stir the roux for the next hour and a half to get it to the deep, nearly black color you want, or you can whisk like hell for the next five minutes on the highest heat you've got. In the end, if it hasn't burned, the roux will be just right. Tonight, the magic was working.

When the roux was finished I turned the heat off under the pot, added the vegetables, and stirred until the sizzling stopped. Then I put in some bay leaves, hot peppers, and other spices and added enough fish stock to fill two-thirds of the pot. Now would come the long, slow simmering required for almost all good food. In two hours I could add the seafood, and ten minutes after that Littlefield and I would be deep into serious eating pleasure.

I popped the cap on a bottle of Dos Equis and picked up Littlefield on the way to the stereo. It was going to be the blues tonight; the only question was which blues I'd start with. Looking through my record collection can take a while. I've been loving music all my life and playing guitar for most of it. Along the way I've managed to collect a little bit of everything I like, and I like the three cousins—blues, jazz, and rock—the best. I picked out Alligator Records' *Living Chicago Blues #4* and was soon enjoying the fine sounds of Queen Sylvia Embry as she wove her lyrics around the heart.

One thing led to another, and after Queen Sylvia had finished, I put on another old favorite, a sweet, sad song called "Tell Me About the Moon." Its singer broke my heart for the umpteenth time:

> Been lonely twenty-one years
> Never had nobody like you
> Been cryin' too many tears
> Never thought I would find you.

I filled my old claw-foot bathtub with hot water, dropped in a linen bag of lavender buds, and lay back to enjoy the bath, the music, and the beer. Missing-persons cases tend to follow you home, though. As soon as I closed my eyes my thoughts wandered

9

around among a restless boy, an old drunkard, and a man of business who wanted one of them for the wrong reasons and seemed to have only a heart full of hatred for the other.

When I got back to the living room I went back to the Chicago blues, and listened to Scotty and the Rib Tips sing about a "big legged woman in a short, short mini-skirt." As Scotty tried to get her to promise to treat him right, I cut the fish up into inch-and-a-half chunks and added them and the seafood to the bubbling pot of gumbo. I warmed up a little rice. That would go into the bottom of my bowl, along with a generous sprinkling of filé powder. My rule about filé is this: If it doesn't make you sweat after the third bite, add some more.

I had two big bowls of gumbo, and Littlefield did his best to keep up. After dinner I stacked the dishes in the sink and put on an old Charles Mingus record I've had for nearly twenty years. I made a cup of espresso and settled back in my ancient recliner with a book by Eudora Welty, who is to literature what Mingus was to jazz. Littlefield came on board toward the end, after the coffee was finished. Soon after that, I fell asleep and dreamed of wandering endlessly along the dusty dirt roads of mid-Depression Mississippi in a bitter and unforgiving heat.

THREE

I didn't wake up until the ravens flew by on their early morning rounds. Their cries jerked me out of a deep sleep, as they did on most mornings. Crows, ravens, blue jays—I love them, but by God they're noisy.

I stretched out some of the kinks in my back—the recliner wasn't all that comfortable—and settled into my morning wake-up routine. I picked my athletic bag off its hook in the back hallway and headed out the door for my daily swim at the Holiday Inn. It's important to be agile in this business, and since I like to eat, it helps that I also like to swim.

I've always been crazy about the water—any water. To me it's a source of life. When I'm stretched too tight, plunging my body into the water is like coming home again. More than once I've solved cases in my head while swimming laps. It's as if the mind is finally free to float without the heaviness of daily life to drag it down.

When I got back home, I attended to the rest of my routine: several strong cups of coffee; breakfast; and the morning paper. I heated up a couple of corn muffins and craved a cigarette while I drank coffee and skimmed through the paper. There wasn't much there—I was used to that—but it's the ritual I like. The letters to the editor were at their entertaining best, though: two ignorant letters about AIDS (it's God's justice), three about George Bush (a fine man under pressure), and one mixed bag whose writer blended amoral, godless, impolite youth with those scourges of civilization who leave their shopping carts in the supermarket parking lots.

"Littlefield would nuke 'em all if given a chance, wouldn't you, Mr. Puss?" He rolled over on his back and grabbed at my hand in a way that wasn't quite life-threatening, although you can never be too sure. Littlefield's evil in the morning.

By eight o'clock the wood stove in the living room was banked, the cat had been let loose on an unsuspecting world, and I was ready to take a drive. I stopped off at the office to check my answering machine and to leave a note on the door in case a potential client should drop by. People are in crisis when they seek out my services and I like to stay available.

The morning was turning out to be crisp, cold, and sunny—a good day to get out into the country, even for a little while. I put on one of my favorite thinking tapes and eased the old Subaru out of the traffic snarl that had already started on the main strip out of town.

There's a problem here with traffic. Even our license plates say we live in "Vacationland," and three seasons of the year we have the Winnebagos to prove it; the trouble is that we still have the same roads that were traveled by horse and buggy more than a hundred and fifty years ago. Now here's a recipe for disaster: Fill these roads with Mom and Pop on vacation and people in pickup trucks checking out the size of their neighbor's woodpiles as they go by; add to this the transplants like me who have no intention of slowpoking it on the highway for the rest of their lives. I solve the problem by rolling the windows up, listening to great tunes, and keeping my nasty comments within the confines of my car. Unless someone learns to lip-read through their rearview mirror, I should live a long and happy life.

Once I was two or three miles out of town most of the traffic was going in the opposite direction. I began to really notice the fine jazz piano playing coming from Mr. John Coates—from "Sleepy-time Down South" to "Mixed Feelings," it sounded like stream-of-consciousness playing, but only John himself knew for sure. His music is so intelligent that when I put it on my IQ shoots up a good ten points. Did I need that today? You betcha.

There are many opportunities to screw up on a case, but to me it's the beginning that stays with you all the way. You come down too hard; you don't come down hard enough; you fail to read a signal; you head off in a wrong direction while your client waits for results that just aren't going to come. I'd done that before but I always stayed mad at myself for a good long while afterward. Hopefully, we learn.

A quick call to my landlord before leaving the office had confirmed the whereabouts of Eugene's trailer and I began slowing down to look for the dirt road that led to it. The road was easy to find and so was the black mailbox on the right, but it would be a good half-mile hike through a couple of feet of snow to get to the trailer. I had forgotten that Eugene wouldn't have a car or a plowed driveway. I pulled the car as far off the road as possible and zipped up my jacket and tucked my jeans into my boots. It was a good morning for a little hike; the air would be clean and I hadn't yet decided how best to approach the old guy. If the boy was there Eugene wouldn't be too glad to see me. If he wasn't there and Eugene didn't know what I was talking about, what then?

Either way, I would soon find out.

There was a bit of a path through the old snow, but no one had walked here since we'd gotten more yesterday. The woods were quiet except for the occasional creak of a branch against a half-fallen old tree, or two gray squirrels chasing each other through their highways along the tops of the trees. A little flock of juncos flew by and a moment later I saw the familiar sight of a nuthatch coming down a tree headfirst. It would've made my head swim but he seemed to like it just fine.

I stood still and for a moment I imagined I was an Indian walking silently through this forest a long time ago, coming back with fresh meat for those who waited in the cold for me. It felt

13

good. Then I rounded a bend and came upon an old and faded pink-and-gray trailer sitting in a little clearing, surrounded by discarded junk from the lives of those who had passed through—a rusted-out old cookstove, skeletons of cars just left to rot when they were no longer useful, old tires by the dozens, and piles of cans and bottles tossed this way and that.

"Oh Christ!" I said, and my heart fell to my shoes. Did we ever muck the planet up but good.

A cursory inspection told me all I needed to know for now. No smoke was coming from the chimney, the windows were frosted over, and there were no fresh footprints to disturb the newly fallen snow. The snow had edged up along the door frame a few inches, so probably no one had opened it to look out at the new morning. Just so as not to overlook the obvious I gave the door a couple of quick raps and then tried the knob once. The place was locked up tight.

One thing was for sure: No teenager was inside and conscious. The kids I knew under eighteen were definitely of the multimedia generation. My own nephew has been known to practice the saxophone with a tasteful background accompaniment of TV, stereo, and radio, which seems like a sort of atonal quartet, at best, to my ears. Even if Eugene just owned an old TV or radio, I was pretty sure I would've heard it if Jesse was indeed there.

I took my time walking back toward the car, trying to make some sense out of this situation. First, where was Eugene? I knew he went into town for his groceries once a week or so. But would he have left his trailer overnight with no heat? Frozen pipes are no joke around here in the winter.

For that matter, where could he have stayed since yesterday? If he had any friends in town they certainly were never with him as I generally saw him, roaming around the streets in his old overcoat with his head down, struggling against the weight of the knapsack that was inevitably flung over his shoulder.

Eugene always had what I call "the look"; that is, the look of a man alone, a man who has been lonely so long he has learned to live inside the space between anguish and despair and this has become his home. I then had a sudden thought: What if this long solitude had abruptly been broken by the appearance of a bright and lively young boy, a boy who had come a long way to call him by the name of Grandfather? Wasn't anything possible? I headed back toward town.

FOUR

"So then what did you say?"

"I said, 'Oh, yeah, Shit-for-Brains? Stick this where the sun don't shine.' "

I was back in my office, laughing so hard my stomach hurt. Molly was holding out the middle digit of her left hand. Her long, bright red nails would certainly give one cause to pause.

"You didn't say that. No way! Tell me you didn't say that to a district court judge."

"Well, I could have." Molly stuck out her bottom lip in a way meant to admonish me, her oldest friend, for not believing every last word that came from her sassy liar's mouth. This time at least, I certainly wanted to believe her. Judge Boynton was the kind of little man who gives all men a bad name. He hated women in general, smart women in particular, and a woman like Molly would have been banished to coldest Siberia if he'd had the slightest chance in hell of pulling it off.

"Well, no. Actually I said, 'Your Honor, could I please approach the bench?' And you know how he talks. He said"—and here she dropped her voice a good octave and slurred her words together—" 'Yes, if you absolutely must, Miss Byrne. But make it short. You cannot expect the court to do your work for you.'

"So I approach the bench and just before I get there I turn around and moon the old fart in front of the whole courtroom. He hasn't seen a butt like this in years, if ever! He takes a good look—I guess he likes what he sees—and has a coronary on the spot and they roll him right straight out of the courtroom and into the funeral home. I said, 'Case dismissed!' "

We were howling like a couple of howler monkeys. I love this woman, but you definitely don't want to mess with her.

In reality, I knew that Molly had inwardly seen red as Judge Boynton had his idea of fun with her in court, but she would've died before allowing him to see her lose her composure on the job. These little flights of fancy operated as a safety valve for her; until Judge Boynton slipped up in public seriously enough to get thrown off the bench—and there were a lot of people who were sure this would eventually happen—Molly was stuck with him. He was alcoholic, racist, sexist, and a lousy card player. Since that didn't stop him from playing in every forty-eight-hour high-stakes poker marathon that came up, he was known to be in hock up to his eyeballs.

"I'll tell you what really gripes my gut, Lil. Simple people—poor people—are constantly being dragged into court for this and that. You know, drinking and getting into fights or digging for clams somewhere when they don't have a license; you know what I'm talking about. It's all small potatoes, really. But they're forced to spend money they don't have in the first place on lawyers and fines. They're having to skip work to horse around with this stuff, but you know what? They should be getting their day in court, their little bit of justice for all their trouble. But then what do they see but this clown of a judge with a red drunk's nose, who'll do his best to find them guilty if he doesn't like their face or their lawyer. It's a mockery of the whole court system. Makes me puke!"

"Not in *my* trash can, you don't. Admit it, Molly: You lawyers are all in this together—hacks, quacks, and ambulance chasers. Here's a joke for you: It was so cold the other day the lawyers were going up the street with their hands in their own pockets." I laughed myself silly while she glowered at me with little slits for eyes. This was one of my favorite ways to get her goat; since she took her legal ethics very seriously, colleagues who skirted the edge of morality were a great thorn in her side.

"Well, we all know the system's full of flaws. I just don't want to be one of them."

I smiled fondly at my old friend. "Amen, sister."

We enjoyed a companionable moment of silence.

"What's on at the movies tonight? Want to go?"

"Can't. I've gotta do a little surveillance jobby tonight. A woman thinks her hubby is cheating—I don't know why, he only goes out five nights of the week. So, anyway, it's my happy duty as a detective to detect where he's going tonight."

Molly smiled at me. "Don't forget to wear your long johns in case you're out all night."

This was a payback for my "quacks" remark earlier. She knew I hated this part of my job; I'm much too squirmy to sit all night in the size of car I can afford.

"Maybe I'll get a car phone so I can call you up and chat when I get too bored on these stakeouts."

"Don't you wish. You'd better get a car that's not an old rust bucket, first." She turned away as if to leave, then started laughing to herself, definitely a bad sign. She turned around.

"You know who I just flashed on? It was the part about the car phone that made me think of her."

I groaned out loud, instantly knowing where she was headed. God, old friends could be such a pain in the ass.

Molly was not to be deterred, though. "What was her name? Dippy? Dopey? Drippy?"

I sat up straight, my stab at a dignified demeanor. "For your information, her name was Dooley, which was a family name. She was a very nice person, by and large, if I remember correctly. She helped me over a rough time."

"Ha! She *gave* you a rough time, if memory serves me well. For two very, very long months—especially for your friends—you dated the Woman from Hell. She used to call you up in the middle of the night during her forty-eight-hour EMC shifts and breathe into the phone. She made you eat tempeh for breakfast, and you had to act like you enjoyed it! I saw you drink some kind of liquid wheatgrass 'shake' and I distinctly remember you saying, in front of me, that it wasn't all that bad. I could tell you wanted to gag. Deny it if you can!"

I had to laugh, in spite of myself. It was an embarrassing story, but one that was true.

"Well, she had charms that you couldn't see."

"And she just *loved* your little Victorian bed with the red Christmas lights strung around the headboard. Am I correct? I do remember you telling me that, don't I?"

I bit my cheek to keep from laughing. Molly didn't need encouragement in this area.

"Well, I might have mentioned it at the time, although the memory is a little dim right now."

"I'll just bet it is. I'd say this reeks of denial."

Once again, Molly turned around to leave. I took a deep breath, having earned one in the last couple of minutes. But she wasn't finished.

"What happened to the little princess, anyway?"

I cleared my throat. "Well, the last I heard she was running some sort of recovery program in Dallas."

Molly nodded. "Yeah, Cretins Anonymous. I think I've heard of that one." She chuckled her way out the door, then stuck her head back in. "You know, now that I think about it, it's been a long time since I saw you that excited about anyone. You should start dating more."

I frowned my surprise, but Molly was gone.

I spent the rest of the afternoon trying to finish up the paperwork, but my concentration just wasn't having any of it. I was much too distracted by a crystal-clear vision of long, slow, luxurious afternoons in that oak Victorian bed, with Dooley's legs wrapped tightly around me, her soft hair and mouth and knowing, experienced hands all over me, claiming every bit of attention I had. I'd been suffering from a broken heart, and she'd been the doctor of love. I hoped she was doing okay in Dallas.

With a sigh, I promised myself to explore romantic possibili-

19

ties soon, and then turned my mind back to the business at hand. I paid the most pressing bills, sent out a couple more, filed some notes from a recently completed case, and took a quick half-hour nap slouched down in my office chair. I was ready for the night shift.

The Dodds' house was a modest white ranch with a black pitched roof, set back from a quiet street a bit by a good-sized lawn. Style-wise, it fit in with the neighboring houses, but its upkeep had obviously slipped, and then some. Paint was peeling off, one shutter was hanging loose at an angle, and makeshift steps led to the side entrance. It looked like the kind of place that could still rally with some loving care and become a family's happy home, but a couple more years of neglect would turn it into a one-house slum for certain. Even the big fir tree in front needed some attention. I could only wonder about the woman and children inside.

The story Libby Dodd told me was this: She and her husband, Bobby, both in their mid-thirties, had been married for fifteen years. They had a boy in junior high and a girl still in grade school. Bobby'd always liked a drink or two with his buddies after work, but he'd come home in time for dinner with the family. This had been his pattern since the kids were small. Then, over the last year, the pattern had changed. At first, once every three or four weeks Bobby would skip dinner entirely. On those occasions he'd arrive home after nine o'clock with the smell of Old Crow on his breath and a string of excuses a mile long. At this stage he'd brought home boxes of chocolates to his wife, along with promises that it would never happen again. He'd appear to follow the straight and narrow for a few weeks, and then, suddenly, would come the missed dinner and the forgotten phone call, followed always by the chocolates.

Over time this pattern, too, had become disturbed; Bobby missed dinner once a week, then twice a week; and for the last couple of months, he was out until late more nights than he was at home. By this time the excuses and the gifts had stopped. Bobby would come home after work to shower and change, often leaving without a word. He was sullen and irritable, and Libby had kept her distance, fearful in the face of his indifference. He had refused marriage counseling and had angrily stormed out of the house when his own father had bluntly asked him just what was going on.

I was clearly this woman's last resort. I could only believe that Libby Dodd had prepared herself to accept the truth and had chosen me, someone she didn't know at all, to confirm what she had long known in her heart.

There was a vacant lot with a FOR SALE sign in front of it just down the street from the Dodds' house. In small cities it's often hard to pass unnoticed on a stakeout—people are used to seeing familiar faces—so I pulled up in front of the lot. This way, I hoped, if my presence attracted any curiosity I would look more like a loose woman on the prowl than a cat burglar casing the neighborhood.

It was six o'clock when I arrived, and here in the North Country this time of year, it's getting toward dark. Bobby pulled up in a Ford pickup truck at six-twenty. "Good," I said to myself, "let's just have a look at you." He sat in his truck for a few minutes with the motor off; then I could see him start to gather up his things to take inside. I stole a glance at the photo Libby had given me. This was the guy, all right.

Bobby Dodd was stockily built, five ten or so, weighing in at about 225 pounds. He had thick brownish hair that had probably been more blond when he was younger. Like many people who marry young and settle into family responsibilities early, he looked and walked like a man older than his age. He had the manner of someone who earns his living with his body, and in cold country like this, physical work can age you and start crippling you young. Whatever his night rambling was about, it didn't seem to be agreeing with him much.

When he was inside the house, I was free to survey my tiny kingdom inside the car. Among my souvenirs were a vinyl-covered case holding ten cassette tapes, a small tape recorder that plugged into the cigarette lighter, a thermos filled with strong black coffee, a bag of potato chips—my longest-running vice—and a large "Italian" sub, by far one of the best regional foods around.

That took care of the entertainment. I also had with me a

21

camera bag containing my Nikon with its paraphernalia, including several rolls of film. The backseat was full of warm things—blankets, extra socks and gloves—and on the dash was the reporter's notebook I preferred to use in the field. It didn't look like I'd forgotten anything, so all I had to do was wait.

Nothing happened for forty-five minutes. In the darkness there was nothing to distinguish the Dodds' house from the others on the block. I could see the glow from a TV set in the living room. The house was warmly lit, and if I hadn't already known some of their sad song from Ms. Dodd, here could've been an American blue-collar success story.

At a few minutes after seven Bobby came out looking freshly scrubbed and got into his truck. I saw the brief flicker of a match before he backed out into the street, heading for his nighttime rendezvous. I started the Subaru up and waited until he had turned the corner before I slipped her into gear. An old favorite song popped into my head and I could almost hear Lou Reed singing in his honey-sleaze voice: "Hey babe, take a walk on the wild side. . . ."

I gave him a fifty-yard lead and we headed across town.

Bobby pulled over in front of a little grocery store on Hammond Drive a few minutes later and left the motor running while he went in. After five minutes he came out with a brown bag the size of a fifth of Old Crow tucked under his left arm. He was carrying a carton of cigarettes. He took a left onto Green Street and followed that all the way to the river. There he turned right onto River Road.

River Road was winding and narrow. It had been quite important at one time, during the days of the big lumber boats. Those days had been gone since the fire that burned down the wharf there over forty years ago. The city had decided not to rebuild for some reason, and River Road was now just another potholed, little-used piece of bad planning.

Bobby slowed down a lot as the road became rougher traveling, so I stopped for a few moments to put some more distance between us. There was very little traffic out here and I didn't want to spook him. When I started back up I couldn't see his taillights, which made me sweat a bit until I remembered the road dead-ended about three miles up.

If I hadn't been going so slowly I wouldn't have been able to see the truck at all. It was all but hidden behind the sizeable wood pile that Bobby had used for cover. The woodpile belonged to a small, shingled Cape Cod set in the middle of a little grove of birches. As I drove by I couldn't help but notice the front door, still ajar, and the couple, feverishly kissing as if this were their last moment on earth. Maybe they were right. These days I frequently found myself wondering why the tragedies of life were so often predictable, and if they were, why we were such helpless, foolish children as to jump head-first, without looking, to our own doom.

I continued on to the dead-end turnaround, in order to find a good place to wait them out. I didn't think either of them would be going anywhere for the next few minutes. I spotted a little lay-by that would suit my purposes just fine. It was well within sight of the house, but not close enough for an occasional running motor to sound any alarms. One advantage of owning an aging car is that most people assume it's broken down if it's sitting on the side of the road. I've yet to see *that* in the private-eye trade manuals.

I turned off the motor and began to organize myself to get this sad little job done. I opened the camera bag first and went through a camera-check routine that was second nature to me by now. First, even though I knew there was film in the camera, I double-checked to make sure. Years ago, the horror stories of two different friends had impressed me to the point of fanaticism on this subject.

I was using infrared film tonight because it's best for night shooting without a flash. I attached the 100mm telephoto lens for distance and the motor drive for speed. The motor drive fits onto the bottom of the camera and allows the photographer to take incredibly fast shots in sequence. It's a little noisy, so a couple of years ago I commissioned a friend who could sew to make a little padded doohickey to fit around the outside of it. I slipped that on and I was ready to roll. I practiced focusing on the front of the house until it was clear and sharp. When anyone came out I'd just have to pick up the camera and it would practically do the work for me.

I sat there with the motor off for a half-hour or so, until the cold began to seep in. Then I started the motor and cranked up the heater as high as it would go. When my feet were a little less frozen I drank some coffee and went to work on the Italian.

Supposedly, these sandwiches were invented in Portland. They consist of long Italian rolls, filled with meat and cheese and slices of bell pepper, tomato, onion, black olives, and pickles, topped with a sprinkling of oregano and good olive oil. They can be a little messy to eat, but that's your price.

For the next three hours I sat there and thought muddled thoughts. Sometimes I turned the heater on and sometimes I saved gas. I tried listening to music but nothing sounded right. My butt went to sleep but the rest of me was wide awake and bored out of what was left of my mind.

At eleven-fifteen someone opened the front door a crack to let the cat out. It was a sleepy-looking, long-haired gray tabby. He pawed the front door a bit and when nothing happened he decided to explore the yard for excitement. After watching him climb up and down two trees and chase after things only cats can see, I started trying to see if I could make him come over to me by using my psychic powers. Either my powers were slipping or he just wasn't attuned to my wavelength, because that was one cat who wasn't interested in leaving his yard.

At ten minutes after midnight the front door opened; I had the window rolled down and the Nikon in my hand by the time they stepped out onto the porch.

She was a pretty woman, about five four, thinnish but shapely, with curly dark hair. I took a whole roll of them saying good-bye, kissing, squeezing and holding onto each other tightly. They didn't look like philanderers, they didn't look like home wreckers; they just looked like two people in love. Bobby didn't even look tired anymore, although I was betting he would by the time he reached home and had to make that long walk from his truck door back to reality.

I let him drive off—I knew he was just going home—and

watched as the woman stood on her little stoop alone, in just her robe and slippers, hugging herself against the cold night air. She watched his taillights disappear and kept looking in that direction long after he had gone. The gray tabby came up and began to curl his body around her legs, doing that little crazy cat dance they all do so well. She smiled and reached down to pick him up. The night was so still I could faintly hear a Randy Travis song coming from inside the house. I could almost hear the purring of the cat as she started back inside the house with him in her arms.

"Sorry it's gotta be me," I said, "but it's time to take care of business." She closed the door and I waited a few minutes before I drove off into the night with her future in my hands.

By twelve forty-five I was sitting at my dining-room table writing my report. Tomorrow morning I'd get the film developed, and an afternoon appointment with Ms. Dodd would finish the case for me. I was glad it hadn't taken too long; I hadn't wanted to charge the woman too much for speaking the words that would in all likelihood end her marriage.

I was also glad about something else. I was pretty sure I could've gotten some cheesy X-rated shots of the two lovers if I'd decided to hang out in the bushes around the house instead of waiting for Bobby's exit and taking a chance on not getting anything more significant than a picture of a truck behind a woodpile. The truth was that I just didn't have the stomach for it. Not in this case. The photos I'd taken would soon speak loudly enough; there was no need to deafen.

I gave Littlefield some milk and climbed the stairs that led to my bedroom. Tonight I was going to try sleeping lying down for a change. My king-sized bed had never looked more appealing. I stripped off my clothes and, for the trillionth time, was grateful I had a home to go to and a bed with warm covers at the end of a long day. I intended to read a little, but my eyes were as heavy as a window that was painted shut. I drifted off into sleep.

FIVE

In the morning I decided to pay Eugene another visit. This time as I walked through the trees I could see smoke coming from the chimney, and as I got closer to his trailer I noticed that the curtains were open and the stoop had been swept more or less clear of snow.

I wasn't sure just how I was going to play this one. He might be a little skittish, but maybe I could turn that to my advantage, with a little skill and some luck.

I gave three good raps to the door and it was opened at once by a surprised-looking Eugene. "Why, miss lady, what're you doing here? Come to see a lonesome old boy?"

"Hello, Eugene. I hope I'm not interrupting anything important, but I was just out this way and thought I'd stop in and say hi to you. Hadn't run into you for a while."

He shook his grizzled old head. "No, ma'am, I ain't doing a thing in this world that I couldn't do better with a good-looking woman in the house. Come on in. Take a load off." He swung the door open wide.

I stepped inside and looked around. Contrary to what I had

expected, the place was pretty neat. It looked like a bare-bones old man's place, all right, but it was more or less clean and some attempts had been made at decoration. There was a mass-produced painting of a man landing a salmon; it was rising up out of the water, having swallowed the bait that would soon prove to be its last supper. Some ceramic knickknacks stood on a shelf dividing the kitchen from the living room: a collie dog being petted on the head by a young boy; a chicken roosting; and a cowboy doing tricks with his lariat.

"Nice place, ain't it." He'd noticed my interest. "It's got all a man needs if he don't need too much."

"It's real nice, Eugene. I should be such a good housekeeper myself."

"Well, it don't have the woman's touch, and that's a fact. But then you'd have to have some woman telling you what you could and couldn't do, and that's the start and finish of a man's problems." He gave me a sly look as if to see how I'd liked his little joke.

"Now, Eugene, I'll just bet you've broken the heart of many a bossy woman." We laughed and he offered me a seat at the kitchen table.

"You'd be wantin' a cup of good hot coffee, wouldn't you? I was just making me a pot."

The coffee reminded me of my grandmother's potent brew. I remembered how she'd leave the pot on the back of her wood cooking stove during the day, and the coffee'd be served to you with condensed milk and lots of sugar. My mother used to say you couldn't cut it with a knife, but I think that's where I developed a taste for strong coffee. I told Eugene as much.

"I reckon my own mama made it the same way, except she used to put eggshells in the pot. Myself, I don't wanna be drinking something that's come out of a chicken's ass, if you don't mind my French."

We laughed together again, and I felt like there was no better moment than now to broach my subject.

"Eugene, how long you been living up north, anyway?"

"Long enough to know I ain't no Yankee. But longer than you, I reckon."

"Oh hell, I'm just trying it out here. Seeing if I can take the winters."

"Well, I've taken quite a few of 'em, but I'd just as soon give 'em back." Again he chuckled at his own joke. I steeled myself for what I was about to do.

"Eugene, I got a call from back home, from a man who calls himself James Cooper. Claims to be your son."

He gave me a startled look and put down his coffee cup, peering into it as if it held all the answers. The old man looked like he'd just been karate-chopped in the throat. I let it wait for a few moments.

"Sorry to spring this on you, but I couldn't think of another way."

The old man sat in silence a little longer, then said softly, "Jim-Boy. That'd be Jim-Boy. He'd be all growed up now."

I couldn't help but feel a certain amount of tenderness toward this man whose past had just suddenly come rushing in on him. He looked frail and vulnerable and his face had lost all traces of his earlier good humor.

"He didn't ever take much stock in me. I don't even know where he is. What'd he say he wants?"

I ignored his question for the time being, and asked one of my own. "So you haven't gotten in touch with your son lately?"

Eugene looked at me as if I were crazy. "How could I? I haven't seen him since he was a half-grown pup."

"Then you weren't aware of having any grandchildren."

I looked him in the eye carefully as I said this.

He slumped farther down in his chair and shook his head no.

I made a quick decision. "Okay, Eugene, I'm gonna give it to you straight. James—who lives in Richmond, by the way—has a sixteen-year-old boy named Jesse. Jesse's been curious about you for a while. Now it seems he's run away from his boarding school and your son thinks it may have something to do with you."

Eugene sat up a bit in his chair. "Boarding school? You mean where rich little shits whose parents don't want 'em go to live?"

I suppressed a smile. The man had a way with words.

"Does that surprise you?"

28

"Damned straight it does. We come from farmers, not big shots. I started farming my daddy's place, what had been my grand-daddy's old homeplace. That's about sixty miles from Richmond, but in those days that counted for a lot."

I had a sudden flash of memory. I was seven or eight years old and we'd been visiting relatives in Richmond, when my mother heard her favorite aunt refer to us on the telephone as her "poor relatives who live in the country." She'd been hurt to the quick and I'd been shocked. We were poor? It didn't seem right, somehow.

Eugene got up and poured us both some more coffee. We sat quietly, thinking our separate thoughts.

"Eugene, what would you do if this boy showed up here at your door right now?"

"He ain't comin' here. He don't wanna see no used-up old bag of bones like me."

"But what if he did? I'm supposed to send him back to his father, you know."

"To his schoolhouse, you mean."

"Whatever." I waited.

"Well, first thing, I'd wanna take a look at him."

"And after that? Would you give me a call?"

"No phone."

"But you can get to a phone, right?"

He sighed, a worn-out sound. "I can do that much, I reckon."

I gave him my card before I left. "Call me, Eugene."

The old man shut his door and I stood there in his junked-up yard for a minute or two, breathing in the cold, fresh air.

In the afternoon it began to snow, big fat flakes that looked like they'd melt as soon as they hit the ground. To my surprise, though, they eventually turned into fine, dry snowflakes that meant business. Once the wind started picking up it began to have all the earmarks of a major storm. I decided to go see Libby Dodd while I still could.

An hour and a half later and I was on my way home. Libby had been expecting me and my bad news, so there wasn't a lot to say. I advised her to get a good lawyer or mediator if divorce was

29

inevitable, or to find a good marriage counselor if she and Bobby wanted to keep on trying. She was a little teary—which was certainly normal, under the circumstances—but in control by the time I left. I felt more than a little sorry for this woman, whose life wasn't going to be on anything like an even keel for quite some time, regardless of how she decided to use the information I'd given her. It might not happen this week or next, but I had the feeling I'd be reading their names in the "Divorces" column of the paper before too long.

It was Friday afternoon and I was much in need of some R & R. With my job I lose a lot of weekends, so a couple of lazy days seemed like just the thing. I stopped off at the store for some groceries and a couple of good bottles of wine.

I've got a little book; it's not black, but it does have some interesting numbers in it. I called one of those when I got home. Misery's not the only one who loves company.

Meanwhile, I plugged in the Stratocaster and cranked up the volume control on my amp. When Littlefield saw me do that he hightailed it up to his favorite refuge in the attic. Littlefield hates rock and roll.

Sunday night saw me relaxed, all nice and mellow, and ever so slightly high. I had a great dinner under my belt, a fire in the fireplace, and some female company that seemed to be staying through the rest of the weekend. What more could a woman need?

When the phone rang, I said, "I won't answer this," and then I said "Shit" rather loudly, but I got to it by the fourth ring anyway. It was Eugene.

"I got somebody over at the trailer you wanna see." I glanced at my watch. It was nine o'clock.

"Give me forty-five minutes, Eugene. I'll be right out. And thanks."

"I just hope to God I'm doing the right thing," he said, then hung up.

I glanced around the room at what I was leaving. "I know what you mean," I muttered crossly.

The drive out took me a few more minutes than I'd thought;

the roads were more or less sanded, but a few icy patches remained. In those conditions you speed only at your own peril.

I used my flashlight for negotiating Eugene's less-than-clear path in the dark. I slipped a couple of times but managed to stay on my feet, which was good enough for this Southerner.

There was no noise coming from the trailer, but it looked welcoming enough. I was cold.

The door was opened by a tall boy who didn't yet have the bulk to support his height. Later on, when he filled out some, he'd probably be a big man. Right now he was a skinny kid who didn't seem to like my looks all that much.

"I don't know why he had to call you. I'm okay."

"Who? Your old man or your grandfather?"

"Let her come in, son. It's cold out."

"Either one!" he said with some feeling. "I don't need this shit."

That was probably true. Jesse finally closed the door after I sat down in my old place at the table. Eugene looked from him to me with some confusion and busied himself with the making of coffee. I took a moment to size up the boy.

He had a good face. Right now he was sullen, he was agitated, and he looked scared, but he had a strong, determined jawline and chin, and big brown eyes that were shaded by long lashes I could only dream of owning myself. I tried to see traces of Eugene in his face, but they weren't apparent in a glance. He was hovering between the door and the table, all nerves, looking like he might bolt any minute.

"This here is Miss Ritchie, son." Eugene threw me a look. "I guess you know who this is," he said to me.

"Hello, Jesse." I tried a brief smile. "Why don't you sit down here with me for a minute so we can talk?"

He hesitated for a moment before taking the seat on the other side of the table. "It's supposed to be a free country. Don't you know that?"

I looked astonished. "Is it? Really? What about all those illegal aliens who're up to their armpits in pesticides? What're they free to

31

do—work for the shit we pay them?" I laughed. "And the home-
less—are they free to sleep outdoors because they like it?"

Jesse leaned back in his chair and looked at me hard. Clearly
this was not the kind of talk he was used to hearing from people
with the occasional gray hair. I'd gotten his attention.

"Look, Jesse. I'm not your enemy here, and I don't know yet
if you have one or not. We can spend all night bullshitting each
other or we can talk this thing out. It's up to you. But you're a
minor and you've involved your grandfather, here. And believe
me, in case you're considering it, being a runaway in the land of the
free is not where you want to go with this."

He appeared to think that over for a few seconds. "Sorry. I'm
not usually rude like this, but . . ." His words failed him and he
shrugged and started tapping nervously on the table with his big
hands.

Eugene set down three cups of steaming coffee and took his
place at the table. "Son, why don't you tell her what you told me."

SIX

"There's this kid at school, Greg. We do things together a lot. Sometimes we go to movies or go out for burgers, things like that. Lately, we started going down to the Fan district to see stuff." A red flush crept up from his throat to his face, finally stopping at his ears. He glanced up at me, without meeting my eyes.

"That's okay, Jesse. I know what the Fan is. Every city has something similar to it. Go on."

"Well, first we went to this pizza place right after the semester started and tried to get some beer. Greg's got this fake I.D. and sometimes it works. It says he's twenty-one. We were pretty nervous, but the waitress didn't even ask us how old we were. So we split a pizza and a pitcher of Bud. Boy, were we drunk. Nobody paid us any attention, though. That's kind of how things started out.

"The next weekend we went there and had this great time again, so we started making a regular thing of it, going there on Saturdays when we could. Then one day we heard these guys talking about a place over on Floyd Avenue where you could buy dirty magazines. We just wanted to see what it was like, you know."

"Hell, son, I've been to many a girly parlor in my life. Man that don't try it don't know much about the possibilities in life." Eugene was turning into quite the cowboy philosopher.

"Sorry, Miss Ritchie. I don't guess I sound like much of a gentleman."

Ah, those Virginia boys hadn't changed much. They still had to worry about being the "gentlemen" Thomas Jefferson wanted them to be, and never more so than when they misbehaved.

"Don't worry about it, Jesse. I've been around the block once or twice myself. What happened next?"

"Nothing much, right off. We tried to kind of fit in, you know, not stand out too much. We couldn't believe some of those pictures! I sort of liked them, but some of them made me feel a little—I don't know—kind of sad and sick, maybe. Well, one day on the way out, this big guy at the counter said that if we needed anything—and he said, 'and I mean *anything*,' we should just let him know. We got out of there fast and started giggling like crazy when we got out onto the street. It was like some cop movie or something."

I knew just where I'd like to drop-kick the kind of creep who would say that to a couple of kids their age. I wasn't going to let my feelings show, though.

"Then what?"

"Well, we went back to school. We told a couple of the guys about it, but I don't think they believed us. We didn't even care; it was like Greg and I had our own world that was a secret from those jerks we saw every day. It was great; at home they think I'm some kind of baby and at school anybody can boss us around who wants to, but in the Fan they thought we were pretty cool, just a couple of guys."

Right. Like bloody hell they did.

I nodded for him to continue. "Just about every Saturday we'd try to go somewhere down around that part of town. Then, a few weeks ago, we went back down to the bookstore. There were more men there that day and we noticed that some of them would go through this curtain into another room. Greg and I waited until no one was looking and kind of ambled over and went

34

through the curtain too. I was half expecting to get grabbed by the big guy and thrown out, but nothing happened.

"There were these booths with thick black curtains in front of them. We could hear sounds and stuff, and voices talking kind of low. We ducked into one of them that was empty. There wasn't anything in there but this machine you were supposed to put money into. We tried a dollar bill. Then this kind of, like, window opened and you could see this lady, uh, well, dancing. She was kinda pretty, I guess, but she didn't look too happy or something. She started dancing like she was dancing for us, too. I mean, she kind of turned our way when she danced." He glanced at me. "She didn't have much on."

"Just her shoes?" I could kind of picture this scene myself.

Jesse looked shocked. "How did you know?"

"Boys aren't the only ones who've seen things, Jesse."

I looked at Eugene, who looked back at me and shrugged. He was smoking one Camel after another and his face had a grim set to it. God only knew what he had seen in his time. "You might as well tell her the rest of it, boy. You're almost there."

Eugene had set the coffeepot on the table in front of us and I filled my cup and the old man's. I looked at Jesse questioningly and he held out his cup. "Thanks. I really like coffee."

"And then?"

"The window only stayed open for a couple of minutes and then this metal cover came down over it. We had a couple more dollars so Greg was getting ready to put one of those back in the machine when we heard loud voices. These men started yelling really loud and we heard things getting knocked over and breaking. It sounded real close.

"I was scared. Greg looked at me and I could see he was scared, too. We kept real quiet as it got louder, and Greg peeked out from the curtain. He didn't see anything, so we decided to run for it. Just as we get outside the booth, this big guy who was usually out front goes dashing past us toward the back. He's got a baseball bat in his hand, and he doesn't look at us or anything.

"Boy, were we scared! We ducked back into the booth. We didn't know what to do or where to go. Then it got a lot quieter all of a sudden. That scared me even more. We heard someone say something about some shipment. One guy said, 'You know I've always been on time before. If I can't get it, you know it's just not available yet.' Something like that, anyway. Then we heard somebody kind of whimpering, like they were really scared to death. Then we heard something that sounded like people scuffling, and then this loud bang. A gun! I'd heard hunting guns and stuff, but this was so loud it hurt my ears.

"This all happened really fast, so I'm not too sure about the exact order or anything, but then we heard some people running and then after that some other people just kind of walking, like they weren't in a hurry or anything.

"After a little bit, when we didn't hear any more sounds, we decided we'd better get out of there too. We were both crying, and I thought I might get sick. When we opened the curtain we saw the big guy lying in the middle of the floor with this knife sticking out of his stomach. His shirt was all red. There was another guy half in and half out of another doorway, who was just lying there with blood all over him, too. He must've been the one who got shot. Neither one of them was moving at all. Greg started screaming and we just ran as fast as we could out of the first door we saw. It turned out that the door led to this alleyway."

At this remembrance Jesse's face seemed to fold as he burst into tears. At this point he looked more like a tender twelve-year-old than like a sixteen-year-old boy who had just seen a shitload of trash. Eugene clumsily tried to comfort him; it had obviously been a while since he had used touch for this purpose, but he was giving it his best shot. I didn't say anything, and after a few minutes Jesse pulled himself together enough to at least look up at me.

"Tell her the last part, son. Then you'll be through for the night. She's a good old girl. Maybe she'll think of something."

Jesse looked at me with something akin to pleading in his eyes. He looked sorely in need of some sleep. He also still looked scared to death.

"Come on, Jess. You're almost there. Just a little more."

He blew his nose on a Kleenex and sighed the shuddering sigh of someone shaken by real ugliness for the first time.

36

"When we got outside there was this big car driving out of the alley really slow. Somebody must've looked through their rearview mirror or something and seen us, because suddenly they braked hard and started backing up toward us. We were so shocked anyway that we hadn't even paid that much attention to the car; we were just glad to be outside in the fresh air. When we realized who they must have been, we freaked out and sort of fell over each other trying to get back inside. We didn't know where else to go. They looked like they were yelling at each other and they looked real mad, though we must've only seen them for a split second.

"We ran through the building and out the front door. I tried not to look at the dead men; I just ran as fast as I could. We ran for five or six blocks, until we had to stop to catch out breath. Then I did get sick. Greg was crying and we were soaking wet even though it was winter and it was cold."

Jesse stopped talking but I could tell there was more. He looked at me, and I could smell fear.

"You wanna know the worst part?" he said slowly, carefully. "I knew one of the men in the car."

A shiver went through me. "Who was it, Jesse?"

"It was Mr. Lukas. He's my dad's partner."

It was long after midnight. Eugene and I had sent an exhausted boy to bed while we mulled over what he'd told us so far. I was smoking one of Eugene's Camels just to remember what it was like. Ex-smokers are like ex-junkies; they don't always hold up to temptation all that well.

There was a lot to mull over. According to the rest of Jesse's story, the two boys had gone back to school and tried to put what had happened at the porn palace out of their minds. I could certainly understand that path of reasoning: Please, God, just make life be like it used to be. The trouble with that is that it almost never works. In my line of work, and in soap operas, nothing stays hidden for long.

It had worked for a few days. Then Jesse had received the usual invitation to Sunday dinner with his parents, which would be followed by a little tennis at the club. Jesse was still enough of a naïve kid to think that his father could grant him some kind of immunity from the outside world. Lukas had been there—charming and casual with Jesse, as usual. Maybe Lukas hadn't really seen Jesse that day. Maybe it hadn't really been Lukas that Jesse had seen. Again, I could see the temptation.

Then, on the following Wednesday, two men had followed Jesse and Greg as they took their customary shortcut through Monroe Park. One of them had held a knife to Greg's throat while a terrified Jesse was made to watch. "You breathe a word about anything you saw and your friend's dead. It could happen anytime, anyplace. And then we'll get you next."

Greg was roughed up but not really hurt; it looked like a warning. It had felt like certain death.

The boys had certainly taken it to heart. They'd sat up late into the night on Wednesday, frantically trying out plans to put their world back together. Nothing seemed to fit anymore. Thursday Jesse concocted his story to the headmaster in an effort to protect Greg. A runaway wasn't going to talk. After all, they hadn't tried to hurt Jesse, had they? Lukas had just wanted him to know it was his responsibility to keep the story quiet.

My blood was boiling. Eugene didn't look all that well himself. This had been one hell of a long day.

"How did Jesse know where you were, Eugene? We never got to that part."

"His daddy had some papers in his desk drawer that he usually kept locked up. Last summer the kid got into the drawer somehow—I guess Jim'd forgotten to lock it that day—and found a report by some private detective. About me. Where I was. Where I am, I guess. . . . Think he wanted to send his old daddy a Christmas card?" Eugene asked bitterly.

"Yeah, right. And maybe some Virginia peaches in the summer."

Eugene laughed ruefully. "Anyway, the boy didn't say anything to his daddy about finding the papers, but he said he'd always remembered where I was. I guess I was like what they call a fantasy."

"We want what we can't have, all right. The main thing is,

it's a damned good thing you were here for the boy. You might have saved his life. I don't know what happened with his father all these years ago, but you're here now. Jesse could do worse."

Eugene looked at me, and for a split second I could see the toll of his dissipated life in his eyes. I imagined a lost weekend that somehow stretched to a lost thirty years or so, lost from everything and everybody who had ever meant a damn to him. Could he just suddenly say, "Yes, now I want to play the game of life"? I wondered.

"Will you be all right, Eugene? We both had better get some sleep; tomorrow could be another long day."

He nodded. "I'm okay—just tired, like you, I guess. I think I can get a few hours' sleep. Do you know what's gonna happen tomorrow?"

I stretched my legs out and failed to stifle a long yawn. "If I had a crystal ball I might. But maybe not even then." I tried to smile at the old man. "Don't worry—I'll think of something."

I knew what my next move was supposed to be; now was the time to call my client and tell him I had found his son. I used the ride back into town to talk it over with myself and we both agreed that it was too soon for that. Suppose Cooper was Lukas's partner in more things than real estate? I didn't know the man, and it would take some kind of monster to be after his own flesh and blood, but some humans are just that twisted. I had to figure out some fool-proof way to be sure I knew just where he stood.

Aside from Cooper's involvement with Lukas, one other problem was gnawing at my gut: Greg. I had to find out if he was safe. Jesse's attempt to take the heat off Greg had been commendable, but the logic of it only went so far. Men like Lukas wouldn't stop at a teenager's show of bravery. Life was cheaper than that. The easiest thing for them to do would be to get rid of the one kid they could lay their hands on first, then take care of the other one when they found him. I had to make sure they never would.

Luckily, Littlefield had kept the bed warm for me—nobody else had. It looked like the weekend was now officially over. I snuggled up to him and he sleepily extended his front leg and paw all the way out to touch my face, claws in, just the lightest feather—one of this cat's most endearing shows of love. Why was everything so very simple with animals, so very complex with the human beast?

I woke up early on Monday, with the barest suggestion of dawn creeping through what was left of the night. I could catch up on sleep later. Littlefield was delighted; usually it took him a good hour to roust me out of bed. He was twitching and switching his tail around so hard I was afraid I'd get lash marks on my leg if he actually caught me with a good one.

I made a pot of espresso and poured it into a thermos and stuck a bagel into a pocket. It would do for breakfast later.

Fifteen minutes later I was doing my laps at the Holiday Inn. The water was a little cool at first, but after a few minutes it felt just right. I swam the crawl for a while, enjoying the feel of the water against my face as I burrowed into it like a newborn at its mother's breast; then the miracle of air when I turned my face ever so slightly out of the water, almost out of breath. Swimming is never monotonous to me—it's my meditation, my freedom as a creature of the animal world after all.

Not a soul was in the pool at this hour. It was still and quiet, with just the sounds of the water and my own breath. Later, little kids would be splashing and jumping, young mothers would be talking gaily, and teenagers would take over the sauna and the Jacuzzi, with radios blaring. No, this was my time of day.

I finished up with the backstroke, feeling as graceful as a swan, and as powerful. After a long, hot shower I drove over to the public boat landing to watch this particular day unfold. I needed to think; and thinking, for me, is not so much frowning and concentrating as it is letting my mind go and seeing what pops into it. That's when things come to me.

I poured a cup of coffee and took a bite of bagel. The sun was up by now, and the ducks and gulls were on the move, getting their breakfast, too. Ice covered the parking lot—I couldn't have gotten in without four-wheel drive—and the ducks were comical as they skidded and slipped on the ice like kids learning to skate. It hadn't been a cold night, and the ducks drank thirstily from little puddles of melted snow and ice that had already begin to form. I made the mistake of throwing out a handful of grain that I keep in the car for them, and the squawk that started from the gulls was loud enough to wake a drunk after a three-day toot.

Mist was rising off the ice floes that were already beginning to crack with the promise of spring. Farther out, I could see where there was more water than ice, and I imagined what it would be like to get into Molly's little boat in a few weeks, drifting along the bay to watch the seals sunning along the rocks and banks toward where the river met the start of the ocean. Then it wouldn't be an uncommon occurrence to watch the bald eagles soaring higher and higher in the sky, waiting for an osprey to catch a fish they'd be able to snatch for a quick free lunch. In spite of the harsh winters, most of us know why we choose to live in Maine.

By the time I finished my coffee, I knew what I was going to do. I had to feel out Cooper, and telephones just wouldn't do. True, he was my client and as such was the man I was being paid to feel loyal to, but a lot was riding on this man's sincerity regarding the kid. If I could trust him, I could always come up with a plan. If I couldn't trust him, I hated to think how much trouble this boy was in.

I knew I must be waking Molly up, but she answered on the third ring. She agreed to put Eugene and Jesse up in a motel we'd used before for this purpose. Cooper could pay me back later. I didn't need to worry about the two of them while I was away. I doubted that Lukas knew the Maine connection yet, but I didn't want to think about what could happen if I was wrong.

I called Cooper next. He must have been sitting on the phone, because he answered it on the first ring. "Mr. Cooper, it's Lillian Ritchie. Hope I didn't wake you up."

"No, you didn't, as a matter of fact. I was waiting for another call to come through, actually. I start my days early, you know." He suddenly seemed to remember how he knew my name. "Miss Ritchie, is something wrong? Have you found my son?"

I decided to take the plunge. "I know where he is, Mr.

Cooper, and he's fine. But for reasons I can't go into now, I can't tell you any more than this on the phone."

Anger shot through his voice. "Just who do you think's paying you, lady? You'd better tell me, and tell me now."

I responded in kind. "I'm no damned 'lady,' Cooper. And what would you say if I told you your son could very well be in danger if I told you any more? What I'm proposing to you is to fly down and see you in person. Then I can tell you what I know."

This calmed his temper down considerably. "Is Jesse really all right? He's not hurt, is he?" He sounded sincere.

"He's really fine, just a little upset and tired. I just need to know if you'll foot the bill if I come down to Virginia. We really need to talk in person. You'll have to decide to trust me or not on this one, but if you checked me out before you hired me you must know my reputation's clean."

"Money's no problem, Miss Ritchie. But if you're screwing around with my son's safety, I'll see to it that you regret it for the rest of your life. Understood?"

"I've always understood that, Mr. Cooper. I'll come by your office when I get to Richmond. Don't tell anyone I'm coming, by the way. It could be dangerous for everyone concerned." That was all I was telling this man until I could see his eyes up close.

"I'll be expecting you. Just get here as soon as you can."

He hung up. I listened to the dial tone and stuck out my tongue at the receiver. "It's 'Ms. Ritchie' to you, fish face."

Now I was free to take off like a fat-assed bird.

SEVEN

I didn't waste any time getting to the airport. They had a flight leaving Bangor International at ten A.M. and I intended to be on it.

The roads weren't really too bad, but then again they weren't so clear that I could exactly speed all the way to Bangor. I ran through the gate just as the last boarding call was being made. Even at that, I managed to snag a window seat. My mother would've called it the luck of the Irish.

I waited for the miracle of take-off before choosing a tape for my Walkman. Soon, as I looked out at that matchless Maine combination of deep woods and water, I was listening to one of my favorite old groups, Cats on Holiday:

> High on the moon
> High on the sea
> High on the starlight
> Follow me. . .

What can I say? This Virginia-based band from the early seventies had knocked me out back then, with its twin lead guitars magically blending melody and harmony. Four of the members wrote the songs that carried us all to another realm, even when the band was having a bad night. They still sounded all right to me. We soared together through the clear sky.

I would be flying into Dulles International. I was grinning to myself. It wasn't lost on me that it took two international airports to transport someone from the North to the South. In many ways, I was sure, they would always be two separate countries, politicians be damned.

To me, Washington and northern Virginia are a sort of neutral zone between the two lands. Whenever possible, I like to fly into D.C. and drive through the rolling hills that define central Virginia and give it its character. It was always a thrill to spot the Blue Ridge Mountains for the first time and see how their gentle presence has influenced the land and the people around them.

Today, unfortunately, I didn't have that option. I needed to do the fastest thing, which meant transferring to a smaller plane that would fly me into Richmond.

On the way to Richmond a flight attendant handed me yet another bag of honey-covered peanuts, which I washed down with some of the worst coffee known to womankind. When I'm finally made Ruler of the World, brown coffee beans will be the first things to go. My highly paid and happy people will cheerfully roast the beans until they're jet black and potent as a snakebite. Children will grow strong and brave under its powerful spell.

Wynton Marsalis and his ensemble gave me the thinking music I needed. I turned the sound down low and tried to prepare myself for all the possibilities I could foresee. I hoped Cooper had been closemouthed about my arrival, or it could mean trouble. I wanted Lukas surprised, not ready and waiting.

The trees below were a light baby-green, that first spring color that quickens the pulse and lets you know that winter has finally gone. In Maine it doesn't come until mid–May some years. Snow and ice were already things of the season past in Virginia.

The warm air hit me in the face as soon as we debarked. Richmond's a little more hot and humid than some of the surrounding countryside, which is, I assure you, not exactly dry. It was a good thing it was only March—I could tell I wasn't used to the heat anymore. Today, I didn't give a damn, though. I felt like any other sun worshipper who has just come out of a long, dark, cold night.

I rented a Chrysler product at the airport, then attempted to remember the correct way to get across town. After fifteen minutes of being hopelessly lost, I pulled into a Texaco station and bought a Dr. Pepper and a map. Richmond had grown so much I didn't recognize a thing I saw.

Map in hand, I not-so-skillfully made my way to James Cooper's office building, which was a high-rise that appeared to be brand-new, overlooking the James River. Riverview Plaza appeared to be a prime piece of real estate, and I was momentarily pissed that I hadn't boosted my rates just a little. A sign in the downstairs lobby indicated where I'd find Dominion Realty and Development, and I took an elevator up to the sixth floor. From there I found my way to their offices, which, I was betting, had one helluva view of a major Virginia river. I walked into a small, tasteful lobby with carpet so thick I watched my weak ankles as I lumbered across it.

A pleasant-looking woman of about fifty greeted me warmly in the reception area. I told her my name and said that Mr. Cooper was expecting me. She used the intercom, and James Cooper came right out, hand extended.

I quickly looked him over. Cooper was a boyish-looking forty-five or so, with curly brown hair that was getting a little thin on top, but was abundant—though graying—on the sides. He was about six feet tall, wiry and lean like a fighter. He had the air of someone who had known a fair amount of success at something. He was wearing an expensive gray suit, but his tie was loosely knotted—his concession to the heat or his casual look, I supposed I could take my choice. He had deep-set, intelligent-looking eyes that weren't giving too much away, save an interested manner.

He was checking me out, too. He'd taken in my jeans and light sweater with a glance that told me he didn't approve of women who didn't cultivate that "feminine" look. I was betting his wife curled, pouffed, and moussed the hell out of her hair. My hair

45

happens to be naturally curly, so I have time to do other things that please me more. I was glad I'd worn my new sneakers; they'd cost me sixty-five dollars and showed a lot of good taste on my part.

Cooper ushered me into his office. The room was typical enough for someone of his position: a large old-fashioned mahogany desk with a massive, comfortable-looking leather chair behind it; a couple of less-comfortable-but-not-insulting-to-the-guests padded chairs across from his desk. The walls were covered with an expensive-looking dark paneling that looked to be the real thing. There was thick carpeting in here, too. A great view of the river below certainly had its points, as did an interesting painting of Confederate soldiers crossing the James on barges. A quick glance at the artist's signature told me Eugene's little boy had come up considerably in the world. I was wondering how.

He offered me a seat. "This is a nice office, Mr. Cooper. You must be doing well."

He eyed me from across the desk. "I work hard for what I get. I'm grateful I've been rewarded so well."

We sat quietly for a few seconds. If it was a who-is-going-to-talk-first contest, I decided to lose graciously. The man had been decent enough to finance my trip down, without knowing what I had to say.

"Mr. Cooper, I appreciate your patience. I'm here to give you the whole story; when I'm finished, you'll understand why I was reluctant to give it to you over the phone."

He shifted in his chair, and for the first time I noticed how tired the man looked. "I must admit, it's been a long few hours since we talked. Could I have my secretary get you anything? Perhaps something cold to drink? There's a canteen down the hall."

"No thanks, I'm fine, really. And anyway, I wouldn't want to disturb your secretary's work."

He laughed. "Ouch—you got me. I guess I'm a sexist, after all."

I didn't say anything, surprised at the turn in the conversation.

"To tell you the truth, it's hard for a guy who was raised in the fifties to know how to talk to women these days. I try, but my wife lets me have it all the time, too. What can I do to get off the hook?"

I laughed too, a little charmed by his candor. "Well, for starters, if you can't call me Ms. Ritchie, you can call me Lillian or Lil. That would help a little."

He nodded, flashing a relieved grin. "Okay, Lil, you've got it. And you can call me Jim; most people do. I'm not that formal a guy."

The tension had abated in the room, or at least most of it, enough to guarantee a better working atmosphere, anyway. Maybe Jesse had gotten some of his good stuff from his dad, after all.

"Now why don't you tell me what all this hush-hush is all about. Where is my son, for starters?"

"Your son believes he is running for his life. I've got him and your father hidden out somewhere until it's safe for them to come out."

Cooper's jaw literally dropped open. I'd never actually seen that happen before. "What? What do you mean? He's just a kid. You said he was safe."

"So far, he is. And I'd like to make it my business to keep him that way."

He whistled softly. "Holy shit. I had the feeling this was going to be bad news." He looked at me with fear in his eyes. "How bad is it going to be?"

"Maybe as bad as it gets, Jim. Some of it depends on you. There may be things involved here you don't want looked at too carefully."

He leaned over the desk, half out of his chair. His face was flushed. "I love that boy, Lil. Some bastard tries to hurt him, I'll rip his heart out. I don't care who he is."

At that moment, I believed him. Whatever faults the man had, not caring for his son was not one of them. He was clean on that account; the rest, I'd have to decide after I knew him a little better. That's why I was in Richmond.

"Okay, I believe you. But tell me something first: Why didn't you report Jesse's disappearance to the cops?"

He threw me a challenging look, one good sport to another.

47

"You tell me yours first. Then I'll tell you whatever's necessary."

It would have to do. I started at the beginning, intending to tell him the whole story and watch him carefully for signs that any of this was already familiar. So far, it didn't seem to be.

I'd gotten to the part where Jesse and Greg had first visited the bookstore, when the intercom buzzed. "Mr. Cooper, Mr. Lukas needs to see you for a moment about that Midlothian property. I told him you were in conference, but it seems to be important. He says it would only take a minute."

He looked at me questioningly and I nodded. I wanted a look at this guy. "Eunice, why don't you tell him to go ahead and pop in? I think he just needs a signature or two from me."

"Is right away okay, then? He seems to be in a hurry."

"That'll be fine. Then no more interruptions, if you can keep the hounds at bay."

She chuckled. "Don't I always?" Then the intercom was silent once more.

Jim apologized for the interruption. "That's okay, these things happen," I said, "but don't say what my job is, if you don't mind. I have my reasons."

He gave me a puzzled look, but nodded. A few moments passed in silence. I could feel all my muscles starting to tighten up, one by one. There was a rap on the door and a man stuck his head inside.

"Jim, I'm sorry. I just need your John Hancock here."

"That's okay, Donny. Come on in." The door closed. "Lillian Ritchie, meet Donald Lukas. Donny's my partner. We started the business together."

Lukas started across the room to shake my hand. I quickly got up and met him halfway. I didn't want him looming over me. His hand was as cool as the rest of him looked.

"Dapper" is a word I never even think of, much less use, but it flitted across my mind anyway. This guy was definitely a looker; my mother would've called him a handsome devil. I'd buy the devil part, anyway. He was around Jim's age, with sandy hair that had a smattering of gray in it. Right now, he was all decked out in a cream-colored linen suit straight out of "Miami Vice," with a pale blue handkerchief and matching hand-woven tie. He was not wearing sneakers.

"I'm so sorry to interrupt your business, Miss Ritchie." He gave me an appraising look meant to charm. "Or should I say 'Mrs.'?"

"I'd rather you just said 'Ms.,' actually."

"Why, certainly." I already hated his smirk.

James Cooper did not appear to be comfortable witnessing our little exchange. He cleared his throat. "Donny, where're those papers?"

"Oh, yeah. Here they are. Bart said to bring them over when I came, so I thought I might as well get this part finished and close out the deal."

"Sounds good to me."

While Jim signed his name in triplicate, Lukas took the opportunity to scrutinize me openly.

"Your face isn't familiar to me, Ms. Ritchie. You are perhaps a client of our firm I haven't met before?"

"I'm considering buying some property downtown. I'm looking around, and your partner has been kind enough to allow me to take up a little of his time."

He stared at me. "Is that right." He was waiting for me to say more, but he could go fish in another stream.

"Okay, Donny. I guess that's everything you needed. Will you be back this afternoon, do you know?"

Lukas pried his eyes off me long enough to look back at his partner. I'd bet money he wasn't used to women who weren't taken in by his load of bullshit. "I'm not sure. Depends on Bart— you know how he is."

Jim smiled at him. "Good luck, my man. You'll close the deal okay; you always do."

"Yeah, I do, don't I?" He turned to leave. "See you, Jim-Bo." He flashed me one last slimy look. "And I'll look forward to seeing you again, too, Ms. Ritchie."

I suspected that might be true. It was enough to make me start locking my windows at night. I nodded at him, but didn't say good-bye when he left.

Jim was looking at me most curiously. "What was that all about? Did you take a disliking to my partner, Lil? He's not that bad a fellow; he kind of grows on you."

Like a fungus, I'd bet. I smiled at Jim. "I don't think we're each other's type. Should I continue with the story?"

He leaned back in his chair, his fingers locked behind his head. "Please. I'm sorry for the interruption."

I told it straight through to the end this time, leaving out the identification of Lukas. I wanted Cooper to take it all in before I slammed him with the final part. His face had paled and his hand shook as he lit up a cigarette.

"Why in God's name couldn't Jesse have come to me? I'm his father. He doesn't even know that old man in Maine. I don't know him myself."

I knew then it was time to tell the rest. "Jim, I've left out something important. I'm trusting you not to fly off the handle and mess things up, now. Okay?"

He looked sick. "There's more? Christ! I thought I'd heard the worst." He smoked a minute, sucking in the blue smoke like it was pure oxygen. I remembered the feeling.

"Okay, give it to me. My son's already witnessed two murders and run off to my old man. How bad could it be?"

I took a deep breath. "The guy who killed those men and threatened the boys . . ." I paused. It was harder to say than I'd thought.

Jim looked me squarely in the eye. "Who? Who the hell is it?" He spoke quietly, but I could feel his pent-up frustration.

"Lukas. Donald Lukas, your partner."

His look was incredulous. "Donny? Come on, Lil! Something's fucked up here. He's my best friend. He wouldn't hurt my son."

"Oh yeah? Why did Jesse identify him, then? Jesse must've known him all his life, if he's as close as you say."

Cooper kept shaking his head no. "I just can't believe this—it's too much. Not Donny. Maybe Jesse didn't see him as well as he thought."

This was the one thing I had feared. I couldn't afford to have

Jim Cooper blow the lid off this thing before I had a plan. Shit! Now what was I going to do?

I had a sudden foreboding. "You didn't tell Lukas about Jesse or about hiring me, did you?"

A dumb, uncomprehending look crossed his face. "Well, sure I told him about Jesse. I was sick with worry; I had to tell someone. I think I might've mentioned you—I mean that I'd hired you." His face turned red. "I don't remember if I mentioned your name or not." He brightened. "I didn't tell him you were coming down here, though."

Shit. So Lukas probably knew who I was all the time. I didn't like it. Meanwhile, I needed to deal with Jim Cooper, who was starting to hyperventilate. His color looked a bit dangerous—pale and greenish.

"Look, Jim, I know this is a big shock to you. Just don't do or say anything until you've had time to absorb it. Jesse could be harmed. And Greg, too, and maybe a lot more people than I know about now. Do you want to go have a drink somewhere until this makes more sense? I could use a beer, myself."

I was fumbling about, trying to buy some time. This man was looking increasingly like the loose cannon we didn't need.

He looked at me as if dazed. "No, I'll be all right. Just give me some time." He made a visible effort to pull himself together. "Can you stay in town tonight, at least? We could have breakfast in the morning and figure out what to do next. I'm afraid my thinking's not too clear right now."

That I believed. I nodded.

"You want me to put you up in a good hotel? I could get Eunice to make you a reservation."

I shook my head. "I'm not very fancy, but thanks. I'll get a room in a motel off 195 somewhere. Should I just call you in the morning?"

"Yeah, that'd be all right." He gave me a card with his office and home numbers. "Just don't say anything to my wife if she should answer. I don't want to worry her."

I gave him one last look before leaving. I wanted to say things like "I'm going to fix this, somehow—don't worry too much," but I couldn't. As I turned to close the door I could see him sitting at his desk, his thoughts already blocking out the world around him. He didn't turn to see me go.

EIGHT

The heat inside the rental car was oppressive, so I opened the windows wide and enjoyed some of my first warm fresh air of the year. I switched on the radio and found an oldies station whose playlist included some of the songs that had shaped my youth. I turned up the volume and listened to Dylan's "Subterranean Homesick Blues," followed by the Animals' "We Gotta Get Out of This Place." The DJ must have been enjoying his work, because he kept adding one incredible song to another, ending up the set with Hendrix doing "The Wind Cries Mary." Good music goes straight to my core.

Traffic was starting to pick up—it was late afternoon—so I made my way to a likely-looking motel. The room was nice enough, cheap enough, and the TV worked. I stretched out on the bed with a Dr. Pepper and watched MTV for a while. I never like everything I see on there, but I always find it an interesting way to find out who's who—who's plastic and who looks real. Rock didn't die after the sixties—there's good music around—but mostly, it's only being played on the rare college or community radio stations.

I drifted off for a while—it had been a long day—and when I woke up it was close to seven o'clock and I was starved. I knew what I wanted to eat, too: barbecued ribs. In the North I can eat health food; in the South, just let me at that good cooking. I headed over to the Fan and found a joint that was just right. It was dimly lit and seedy-looking, and had old Hamm's Beer signs on the walls. I ate my fill of ribs, potato salad, beans, and cress, and washed it down with a couple of Rolling Rocks. The black woman who ran the place also controlled the jukebox, which was a good thing for us all. She played Aretha, Aretha, and more Aretha. I didn't ever want to go home.

It was nine-thirty when I pulled up to my parking space at the motel. I was glad I'd gotten a room earlier; the place, at least judging by the number of cars in the lot, was filling up fast. I love motels. The room already felt homey and familiar. The TV was beckoning. I watched a nature show about sea turtles, followed by a terrible remake of a great old movie. Around midnight I fell into an exhausted sleep.

I woke up in pain and terror. The room was completely black, but I could see stars, all right. Someone's hand was over my mouth and partially over my nose, blocking my breathing as well as my screams. I thrashed out wildly, my lungs desperately in need of air. Someone slammed a punch into my gut that felt worse than anything since B. D. McDowell hit me in the same place in fourth grade. Only now, there was no Cousin Billy to beat the shit out of him later.

The guy holding my mouth shut tried to hold onto my left wrist with his other hand, his knee digging into my right arm so successfully it was entirely out of commission. Luckily for me, I'm left-handed and I have a fair amount of strength. I wrenched my arm free and slammed wildly at his face—the closest target—then pulled his nose as hard as I could. That effort got me a punch to the jaw that made me nearly black out.

I was dimly aware that someone was trashing the room—I could hear stuff being thrown around and glass shattering. I could smell the rank sweat of the man, or was that the smell of my own fear? A couple of punches later and I'd stopped resisting—I could take a hint—and waited for them to do whatever they were going to do. I was alone and beyond hope. I remembered, bitterly, my Walther PPK, locked, as usual, in its case at home, where it could do no one any harm or any good.

Suddenly, I realized the beating had stopped. One of the men grabbed me by the jaw and squeezed. "Stop your snooping, you Yankee bitch. Go back home."

I waited, tensed, for a last punch that never came. I heard the door close a few seconds later. One of the men said something that made another one laugh, then I heard car doors slamming shut. I lay there, crying tears as bitter as bile, a casualty of the night shift.

For a while I drifted in and out of consciousness. I'd wake up and think, "Call 911," or I'd wonder for a split second if I could sit up and move around. Then I'd realize I'd drifted off again in between. Finally I made myself try to sit up—that would at least prove to me that I wasn't dying—and after a couple of tries I was able to switch on the light over my bed. It was two o'clock. My clothes were strewn all over the room, as were my books and papers. The rest of the room looked like shit, too—drawers taken out of the desk and thrown around, chairs knocked over, a lamp broken.

Everything hurt. Breathing hurt, swallowing hurt, and staying conscious hurt most of all. Finally, I creaked and swayed my way into the bathroom in time to lose the remainder of my dinner. I splashed some water on my face and looked into the mirror. There was blood from a cut on the lip, and a cheekbone that was already beginning to puff up. My gut hurt like hell, and so did my *hair,* for that matter. My own eyes stared back at me crazily; until a few minutes ago, I'd thought I was going to die.

I flopped back on the bed, shaking all over, soaking wet with perspiration. I wanted nothing more than to go back to sleep and to wake up with another, more simple life. Something functioning as my brain told me that wasn't such a good idea—I could die of internal injuries. Somehow I found the card James Cooper had given me and dialed his number. Calling 911 would have alerted the cops, and I wasn't in any mood for cops.

He answered right away. "Jim, this is Lil. I need some help."

He sounded alarmed. "Are you okay?"

That was a good question. "I hope so—I love me a lot."

His voice rose in pitch. "Are you hurt? Did someone hurt you, Lil?"

"Yeah, I guess they did. I think you'd better drive me over to emergency; I don't think I can make it by myself. I'm a little woozy."

"Sit tight, Lil; I'll leave right away."

I doubted I'd be going anywhere, meanwhile. "I'm at the Regal Court Motel, off 195. Do you know it?"

"It's the old one, right? With the funny windows?"

"That's it. I'm in Room Nineteen, around the back. Get here soon, okay?" I hung up the phone.

As out of it as I was, I still knew a drunk when I saw one. Jim Cooper screeched up to the parking lot and jumped out of his Volvo station wagon twenty minutes later. I opened the door for him, and his breath could have knocked me down, not that it would've taken all that much in my state. His eyes were bloodshot and his shirt was only half tucked in. Fine, I thought, we'll look like one charming couple.

He winced when he got a good look at me. "Oh shit, I'm sorry, Lil. Oh God. I really am. I mean it, Lil, I really do."

I felt like speaking with God a bit myself. First thugs, then a drunk—what had I done to deserve this?

"I don't think it's as bad as it looks. If they'd wanted to kill me, they had the perfect opportunity. I just want to make sure nothing's broken or leaking." All that talking hurt.

Jim still couldn't take his eyes off my battered and bruised self. "Don't worry, Lil. I'll get you there in ten minutes, max."

I looked at him warily. "Can you really drive? You look like you fell into the bourbon barrel."

He straightened up a bit and partially tucked in his shirt. "Don't worry. I'm a Virginia gentleman first and foremost, and I've always been able to hold my liquor."

How, I thought nastily—bottoms up? I sighed. "Okay, let's go, but I'm warning you: Get me killed and I call my lawyer."

I closed my eyes as soon as I was settled in the car; if we were

56

going to crash I didn't want to see it coming. I also wasn't up to talking yet. I needed a dose of painkiller, and I needed it fast.

Jim careened right up to the emergency-room door, and a man and woman in white immediately put me on a stretcher and wheeled me into a cubicle with all kinds of machines. The doctor was young and had soft, worried brown eyes.

"What happened to you, Ms. . . ." He looked around for a chart that hadn't arrived yet.

"It's Ritchie, but you can call me Lil. I always say that to people who're saving my life." My own voice sounded strange to me, too husky, a little slurred.

He smiled, but his pretty brown eyes showed concern. "What did you run into, Lil—a semi truck?"

"A couple of 'em. How'd you know?"

His hands and fingers touched me here and there, gently. He shone a light into my eyes. He listened to me breathe. I tried to do it well. We didn't talk again until he had finished checking me over.

"Did your husband do this to you, Lil? Because if he did, he must be stopped. You could file charges and the police could pick him up right here."

I laughed in spite of the pain it caused. "You mean the man who brought me here? God, no. That's not my husband, and perish the thought. I just ran into some trouble that's all taken care of, now."

The doctor shook his head sadly.

"Honest, Doc. I don't have a husband. And if I did he'd be a dead one by the time I got through with him. That man in the waiting room is an acquaintance who's simply trying to be kind. Really."

My savior in white—his name tag said Dr. Greenstein—kept looking at me sadly for a moment, sighed, and wrote something down on a pad. I figured he must see a lot of this shit.

"Lil, I'm sending you down to X ray for a couple of pictures of here"—he touched my tender stomach—"and here"—and his hand grazed the air over my cheek. "If nothing's broken—and I don't believe it is—you'll be able to go home tonight. I'll give you a prescription for some Tylenol with codeine that'll look after the pain. Take it easy for a couple of days, though. Your body has a lot of repair work to do."

In less than an hour my clothes were back on and I was hobbling out with a much more sober Jim. This time he reeked of coffee, cigarettes, and bourbon, in that order. It was a start.

Somebody was going to pay for this, and dearly. I shivered in spite of the warm night.

We stopped at the first all-night drugstore we saw, and Jim held out his hand wordlessly for the prescription. A few minutes later he came out, painkillers in hand. He had also bought me a little bottle of grapefruit juice; I had all the makings of one hell of a perfect cocktail. I had swallowed three of the pills and downed most of the juice before he spoke.

"Lil, what exactly happened?" His face looked drawn and tired, all the effects of the liquor gone and forgotten.

"You don't know?" I turned around to face him. "Why don't you tell me? No one knew I was here but you." All of a sudden I was mad as hell.

His face drained of all color. "You don't think I did this, do you? My God, Lil, I'm not a violent man."

I sighed. From the little I knew of the guy, I couldn't see it happening that way myself. "I think you must've let my name slip to Lukas earlier, then. The goons who beat me up called me a Yankee bitch, and the room was too dark to see my identification. Lukas must've had me followed after I left the office. I guess they just waited until later so they'd be less likely to be seen."

Jim slammed the dashboard with his hand. "Shit. It's all my fault."

I closed my eyes for a minute or two. I felt like I could use about three weeks of good solid sleep.

"That's not gonna change anything, Jim." I opened my eyes reluctantly. "Can you come up with a cup of coffee? My brain's not working too hot right now." It was true; my night had more than caught up with me.

A few minutes later we were tucked into a Naugahyde booth

in a diner that had seen better days. I tasted my coffee; at least it was good and strong.

The painkillers had started to work; I felt a distance that was comforting, but more than anything I longed for a soft pillow. This was not to be, however. I made myself sit up straighter and look at Jim.

"Do you finally believe me? Because if you keep defending your pal Lukas, I don't know what I'm going to do with you." I meant it.

He looked down and fingered a deep scratch in the Formica table. "Yeah, I believe you. I hate myself for it, but that'll probably pass. I'm used to feeling loyal to the guy, is all. Twenty years is a long time. I thought I knew him."

"So did Jesse. That's got to be your main concern now. The guys who beat me up are probably the same two who scared Jesse into running away. Think about that when you feel sorry for Lukas."

"Do you think someone's looking for Jesse right now?"

"I'm almost certain of it. Things have gone too far. Why don't you call the police? They've got the people to deal with this. I'm working alone, here."

He didn't say anything for a bit. When he did, I could see four in the morning written all over his face. I knew this hadn't been his only sleepless night of late.

"I can't deal with the cops, Lil. It's a long story."

"Then make it short. I'm not a cop. I'm certainly not going to turn you in for anything."

He thought a minute and then nodded his head. The waitress gave us some refills and he waited until she left before starting to talk.

"Donny and I got back from Vietnam in '70. It was a hell of a time to come home if you wore a uniform. We'd seen some shit you couldn't even imagine. I mean it, Lil. I still have nightmares. Suddenly here we were, back home, and everyone we saw was either embarrassed by us or pissed off at us. In uniform, we couldn't even get waited on sometimes. It didn't take us long to realize we had to put this shit behind us, and soon.

"I'd been into drugs over there a little bit, nothing major though. I smoked a lot of pot in those days, but I knew some guys who were into a lot heavier stuff."

I thought back. "Heroin?"

"Yeah. I'd read enough about horse to know it wouldn't get you anywhere but dead in the long run. I didn't fool around with that shit."

"Did Donny?"

He hesitated. "Yeah. I didn't know how much until we got back home. By 'home,' I mean San Francisco. We kicked around there for a while."

Me too, but not for the same reasons.

"One night we'd been out listening to music—there were some great bands around there at that time—and we'd had a lot to drink. Donny said he knew a way to make some real money. I said, not thinking, 'Without getting busted?' Donny just laughed and laughed, so I knew it was something crazy. The guy's a kind of genius, Lil. He can make things work—things that I wouldn't even think of, much less pursue. Anyway, he had connections already set up to smuggle a lot of heroin into the country. He wanted me to help him. He promised me, and I believed him, that this was a onetime shot. We would use the money to start a legitimate business, and it would be put behind us as soon as the deal was over."

I was all ears, my pain and tiredness forgotten. "Was it?"

"I thought so. It certainly was for me. Underneath I was always just a Virginia country boy. I only wanted to salvage some kind of a life for myself. I didn't want to carry around bitterness about the war until it killed me.

"We came back to Richmond and started looking around for a business of some sort. Real estate was just beginning to be big—you could smell the money. Richmond was really starting to grow and I knew we could be in on it. Within the year I had my license. Donny got his around the same time. We started off in a little building near the Fan. We got it for cheap and had plenty of money left over for operating expenses. We'd accomplished our dream. I married Ruth right after that. She was a hell of a catch, believe me.

She's a good woman, too good for me. I knew we could make a great life together. I needed that.

"Jess was born in June of '74. It was the happiest day of my life. I could finally leave my crummy childhood behind, leave the lousy war behind, and just concentrate on being a good husband and father. I hadn't seen it up close, ever, but I knew in my bones what a good marriage was all about. God, how I wanted that."

I could see he meant it still. "So what went wrong?"

"Nothing. It was like none of it had ever happened—I mean with the heroin. We ran a clean business, we worked hard, and we've done well. It's the American ideal. It's just that I can't get the image of those body bags stuffed with dead soldiers and heroin out of my mind. Some nights I've woken up dripping wet, with my heart pounding."

"What about Lukas? You ever talk it over with him?"

He looked grim. "Just once. I wanted to somehow give some money back—I felt like a cheat—and I wanted to tell my wife the whole thing. I felt like no good could come out of such a sleazy start. I felt like an impostor."

"What happened? Did Lukas have similar pangs of conscience?"

He shook his head. "He laughed in my face. He thought I was an utter fool. Finally, when he couldn't convince me I was wrong, he showed me a document he's got squirreled away somewhere that has my name connected with what we did. His name wasn't on it anywhere, of course."

I was incredulous. "And you kept being partners with this guy? Couldn't you have gotten out on your own and started over again, without this noose around your neck?"

He couldn't look me in the eye. "It's kind of complicated, Lil. I love the guy, for starters. I know he's a little crazy, but a part of me admires him for playing by his own rules. I also thought I could keep him clean. Pretty soon it was out of my mind altogether, except maybe late at night a couple times a year. We all have little corners that aren't swept all that often. You must have a couple yourself."

I wasn't in the mood to talk about my dust balls at the mo-

61

ment. "So you like and admire the guy in spite of yourself—am I getting it right?"

He nodded. "And does Lukas have similar feelings for you?" I wanted to get this straight.

He shrugged. "We're friends—I can't explain it, but it's like we were brothers or something. He's like the older, braver brother, and I'm the tagalong younger one, I suppose. His family was as fucked as mine, growing up, and somewhere along the way we just got into this way of being with each other that satisfied both of us, I guess."

"Yeah, well, he's threatened to kill his only brother's only child, then. How does that fit in with the rest of your picture?" I could stand only so much alpha-dog talk.

Jim looked so miserable I was immediately sorry for my sharpness.

"I don't know. I guess he's backed into a corner with this. I certainly didn't know anything about the porno stuff, and I wish I could say I'm shocked, but somehow I've always known that he's capable of doing some heavy shit. I just thought, naïvely, I guess, that I could be the guy with the white hat who'd change his mind when the time came. He told me once he hadn't minded the killing in Nam all that much. I think it excited him."

He shuddered and shook his head fiercely. "Jesse can't be in the way of a Donny who's desperate. That Donny could do most anything."

I nodded. Lukas sounded like one sick, sorry son-of-a-bitch to me. "And Ruth—she still doesn't know anything?"

"Not a thing. I've been a gutless wonder, huh?"

"Mine is not to judge; it's to keep anything worse from happening. What about Jesse? She must be worried to death right now."

A quick flush ran up his neck. He hesitated, then started to speak. "Well . . ."

Suddenly I saw where this was heading. "She doesn't even know Jesse's missing, does she?"

He shook his head. "I told her he'd forgotten about our

dinner and had made plans to go to Greg's uncle's house for the weekend instead."

I sat there shaking my head, myself. We must've looked like a palsy convention. Guys! Did they imagine all women were brain-dead, or what?

"You're gonna have to talk to Ruth, Jim. She must know something's wrong, believe me. She's got to. I can't protect Jesse without her knowing what's going on. She could be tricked into telling Lukas something he shouldn't know. Go home and talk to her. Do it now."

He rubbed his eyes and face with his hand. He took a deep breath. "Yeah, I guess you're right. It's time, isn't it?"

"Don't wait until morning, Jim. It could be too late. Lukas knows who I am, he knows why I am here, and to judge by the beating I got, he knows his cover's blown. I doubt he thought I was so stupid I wouldn't figure where the goons came from. He may be out of town already, headed toward Jesse. Time's up, Jim—you've got to come clean to Ruth. I'd also advise you to talk to the cops."

He shook his head violently. "I can't. They start looking into Donny, they'll look hard at me and see what a house of cards it all is."

I thought about it for a minute. I didn't like it, but maybe just until Jesse was out of danger . . .

"Okay, Jim, but you'd better think about what's gonna happen when the rest of the shit hits the fan, because you can bet your ass it's gonna."

A yawn escaped, and suddenly I was cross-eyed with exhaustion. "How's about you check me into another motel? I need some shut-eye, and I'm sure not going to sleep in that bloody room. We could pick up my stuff on the way."

He nodded, eager to please. I could see how Lukas had used this man's basic goodness to his own advantage.

"I've been wondering about something. How'd you know about me, anyway? I never did ask."

"Gordon Black. He uses a P.I. every now and then, and I asked him if he knew of any in Maine. He handles a few divorces and sometimes deals in custody cases where one of the parents live out of state."

I smiled. Gordon had sat behind me in a high school book-keeping class, where we were both known to doze off. I wondered how he'd managed to stay awake through the rigors of law school.

"Thanks for tonight, Jim. You did okay."

He stretched out his long legs and stood up. "Yeah, I'm good in a crisis, all right—after all, I'm experienced. I've been to war, you know."

A war that wasn't over by a long shot, I thought. I got up slowly, plenty sore in spite of the medication. We left the diner.

Outside, I looked up. The morning light was finally beginning to block out the stars.

It was close to ten by the time I managed to drag myself out of a drug-laden sleep. I opened my eyes warily—oh yeah, I was in the Holiday Inn—and sat up. Now *this* was class. The room was spacious and very clean; I could probably even walk around safely without my slippers. I tried to stretch, but my body said a loud and resounding no. Damn! Someone really was going to regret having done this to me. "Little creepy coward bastards," I said, "just try me sometime when I'm standing on my feet."

I called Jim at the office first thing, and was told by Eunice that he'd taken the day off and to call him at home. That didn't exactly surprise me. I asked casually if Mr. Lukas was in yet and she said no, but she was expecting him any minute. I had the feeling she'd be waiting quite a while.

I called the Cooper household next. Jim answered right away, sounding as sleep-laden as I felt. He yawned into the mouthpiece of the phone. "Sorry, Lil—I was up all night. Ruth and I talked well into the morning. Then we were too tired to sleep. You eaten?"

"Now that I think about it, no. I'm a breakfast woman, too. You?"

"Nope, not yet. Hold on a minute." He put his hand over the phone for a minute and then said, "Why don't you come on over here and we can fix you a real breakfast. We've got sausage from a farmer Ruth knows, and I'm a pretty good biscuit maker. You and Ruth need to meet, I think."

"Is it hot sausage?" I asked. "Because I hate that mild, sissy stuff."

He laughed. "Do you know how to get to our house?"

"I had an aunt who used to live in Windsor Farms. I think I can wing it." We hung up.

I took a cab over to pick up my rental car, carefully avoiding the person at the front desk; I didn't feel like explaining whatever mess remained in my old room, though Jim and I had done our best to restore it to its tacky neatness when we'd picked up my stuff.

"Windsor Farms" didn't mean it was in the country. I'm not sure where the name originally came from, but it now stands for an old residential section filled with stately homes built near the turn of the century. As I remembered it, there had been a ritzy section of town for Jews first, and Windsor Farms had been built by the WASPS, who felt jealous. In the days of segregation, at least, the few blacks who inhabited the area had come in through the back door, holding groceries and brooms.

I found the Coopers' house with very little trouble. It was a two-story white brick that had a nice shape to it—not too boxy for my taste. What I really liked was the trees. A huge old oak towered over the house—it must've been old enough to have seen the Civil War—and around the right side, by the screened-in porch, was a beautiful, healthy-looking magnolia. There was a black walnut tree in the back yard. This being Virginia, boxwoods cuddled up against the front of the house, a fortress of little green leaves. Various gardens took up space in different sections of the yard; something that looked like an herb garden was to the left, and a rose garden was off to the right side of the house, near the magnolia. They either had one hell of a gardener they paid for this, or one of them had put in a lot of work and did a lot of upkeep.

I would've loved to have seen this place when the roses and the magnolia were in bloom. I was sure the roses would be of an old variety—much like my grandmother's—and for a moment I savored the thought. The long winters of Maine leave me starved for the lush Virginia springtime, full of its promise of summer. It was hard to imagine that the residents of this lovely home could have such a cloud of trouble hanging over their heads. I rang the bell.

The door was opened at once by a woman who was around my age. She had reddish-blond hair cut in some sort of sweep that looked easy to take care of. Her eyes were blue and lovely to look at, and her skin was on the fair side, with freckles on her cheeks and nose. Her hands looked strong and capable. If she hadn't been the wife of a real estate guy she could have been living on a farm somewhere in Albemarle County, raising horses and loving it. I knew I had found the gardener in this house. I liked her on sight.

She smiled at me and offered her hand to shake. She had a warm and friendly grip. "Ah," I said to myself, "the light in Jim's life." No wonder he'd been afraid to lose her. Unlike me—and unlike Jim, I realized when I saw him—Ruth Cooper didn't show how tired she must have felt. The woman looked to be made of sturdy stuff.

She led me back to the kitchen, which was filling up with smells that made my stomach growl. Sausage was slowly cooking on the stove, and coffee was dripping in a coffee maker that looked like it could do a trick or two. Was that a nozzle for making the steamed milk for cappuccino? My stomach gave another, more audible growl. Biscuits were all rolled out, waiting for the oven to do its magic. Jim was busily beating the eggs that would be scrambled at the last minute. This domestic scene would have seemed entirely inappropriate if I hadn't known about Southerners and breakfast.

Jim looked up at me with a look that was both concerned and amused. "You don't look all that bad, considering. You must be as tough as pig iron."

"I wish I could say the same for you. You look like bloody hell." Ruth laughed. It was true. The guy had traveled back and forth over twenty years in less than twenty-four hours, and it showed.

Ruth put down a cup of coffee in front of me. I inhaled deeply—it smelled pretty damned good. Maybe Jesse could stay with Eugene and I could move into his room.

The thought of Jesse suddenly made me feel even more tired and sore. Today was the day I had to put a plan into action, before it was too late.

The three of us wolfed down a breakfast that could've fed the same number of lumberjacks. None of us said much, beyond the polite necessities, until we were finished and had fresh coffee in front of us.

Ruth spoke first. "Lil, Jim has told me everything. I know that Jesse is all right for now, though it hurts the mother in me not to be able to see it for myself. What are you proposing we do?"

"First of all, we'll call Jesse in a few minutes, so you can see for yourself how he's doing." I took a deep breath. "Last night—this morning, really—before I went to sleep I did come up with a plan. It might sound farfetched, so you'll have to trust me enough to hear me out. Then if you don't want to do it, we'll start over from scratch." I looked both of them in the eye. They looked back. I took it as a good sign all around. Ruth took her husband's hand and laid it on the table, intertwined with her own. Jim said, "Lay it on us. We've got to do something."

"Okay, here's what I was thinking. First of all, we've got to get Jesse and Greg far enough away that Lukas can't get to them. It's hard to tell how many feelers Lukas has out, and to my way of thinking, we've got to get the boys away from any curious eyes." I looked at Jim. "Does Lukas know about Eugene?"

He thought a few seconds. "Yeah, I used to bitch about him to Donny. He knew when I had him traced." His expression told me he had already sifted through all the implications. I tried to convey more certainty than I felt.

"A good friend has put Jesse and Eugene in unofficial protective custody, which is the best we can manage, for now." I looked into their stricken faces. "I understand your concern, and I really believe they're safe, but we have to act fast."

Jim nervously bit his thumbnail down to the quick, but Ruth sat calmly and quietly. "Do you have any way of finding out if Greg is okay?" I asked her.

"He was all right yesterday, because he called here to see if Jesse was visiting us." She glanced sidelong at her husband. "Now

I know he must've been worried to death." She thought a minute. "Greg has an uncle. His parents are dead—some automobile accident when he was small—so his uncle raised him. He's an older bachelor with a lot of inherited money. He cares for Greg in his way, I think, but he's never really known what to do with him. He's had him in boarding schools since he was small."

"Okay," I said, "that may work in our favor. My plan is to get back up to Maine as fast as possible and grab up Jesse and get him the hell out of Dodge City. The jerks who beat me up have to know who I am and where I live, so Maine's no good as a hiding place for long. I've got friends and connections out West—maybe for now it's better if I don't say exactly where—and I think I could keep everybody safe there. We've got to get Greg out there, too, somehow. The spaces are more wide open, and I've got old friends who, believe me, can be counted on in a pinch. Meanwhile, Jesse and the others will be out of the way of any Virginia heavy guys." I paused and caught my breath. "So what do you think?"

Jim spoke this time. He looked thoughtful. "How would you get out there—fly?"

"No, that's too easy to trace from an isolated place like northeastern Maine. I was thinking I would rent a car in Boston or Portland and slip up and get Jesse and Eugene. Then I could drive down to New York and get on a plane with them from there. No one will be expecting a move like that, I don't believe. I think that might give us some valuable time to get set up before Lukas makes his next move."

I looked carefully at Jim's and Ruth's faces. They weren't closed to my idea. "I know this sounds a little off the wall, but I'm sure it could work. As long as Lukas is where he's comfortable, he's got the advantage. I don't want anyone getting hurt who shouldn't be. I don't know how to get Greg to join us, though. I was hoping I'd think of something, but—"

Jim interrupted me. "I don't think you should fly at all."

Ruth and I exchanged glances. "Why not?" I was puzzled.

"Donny's got all sorts of connections in the airlines. I know he has pilot friends; he dates stewardesses a lot. I know it must seem

68

paranoid or something, but I'd just feel a lot better if you bypassed that part. You could drive all the way out, couldn't you?"

I shrugged. I'd certainly done it enough in the past. "I don't see a problem. Maybe it would be a good idea—we don't know who's on his payroll, after all. I wouldn't mind."

"Good," Ruth said. "Then I could take Greg to meet you somewhere along the way. Say, at a prearranged spot in D.C. or something. How would that be?"

Jim was staring at his wife in wonder. "You? You'd take him? Why not me?"

"Because Donny Lukas will definitely not be expecting me to do it. Whereas *you*"—she smiled—"he could predict your every move. He knows you entirely too well."

Jim looked doubtful. "Couldn't he follow you when you pick Greg up and knock you in the head or something?"

"He could knock you in the head easier—he's not afraid of you. You'd probably turn around to give him easier access."

Jim rolled his eyes in embarrassment.

"Actually, Donny *is* scared to death of me, though I've never told you this before, Jim. One night he tried to hit on me in the kitchen when you'd gone out for a few minutes. That was the second time it had happened, and I told him some things very clearly. He's given me a wide berth ever since. The other thing I'd have going for me is that he thinks women are stupid; it would never occur to him that I'd be doing something like that. Think about it and you'll know I'm right."

Jim appeared to do just that. He looked at me. "You know, it's crazy enough that it just might work."

I nodded. It had the right kind of feel. "Will we tell the uncle the truth or lie like dogs? I don't want a kidnapping charge on my head—it'll be hard enough as it is."

The couple looked at one another. Ruth spoke.

"The uncle's pretty stodgy—he'd never knowingly go along with the plan. I'm afraid of what'll happen if he gets mixed into this. He's pompous and used to giving orders right and left. No, we'd better do it our way and tell him later. I'll take full responsibility with him, Lil."

"Meanwhile, what do we tell him that'll get Greg out of school and into my car?"

Ruth was on a roll. "I'll call him right away and tell him how we're sending Jesse on a cultural trip of some sort and we'd love to have Greg along too. Believe me, he'll be more than glad to give the boy to us. Greg spends the little time he's at home with housekeepers and servants, for the most part. His uncle travels a lot. He'll get his secretary to call the school and tell them to release Greg from his studies for a few days, and that'll be it. When Hugh Randolph speaks, you'd better believe Orton Academy listens."

She seemed to have said her piece. I asked, "Can you foot a big bill, Jim? All this traveling about's not cheap, and my expenses will be high. We may as well be realistic."

"Sure, that's not a problem. Just make it work out and it'll be worth that, and more."

"I'll need some operating cash, then. Now's no time to be using credit cards or checks."

"I'll just run over to my bank before you go. I'll get out more than enough for now, and I can send you more any time you want me to. This is my kid we're talking about here, and I'll do whatever's necessary to keep him safe."

"I've got a question," said Ruth. "What if Donny shows up? Could he have just walked away from the company? That seems too simple."

"I think he'll be lying low for a little while, is all. He'll probably call in to the office with an excuse for his absence, for now. After that, he'll be waiting to see who knows what. I don't think you have to worry about him thinking nothing's changed. If he knows you hired me, and guessed that I've talked to Jesse, he'll be too worried about what's going to happen next to hang around here watching Jim's face for clues. It's too late for that. He blew his cover, as far as I'm concerned, when he sent his boys over to my motel last night and they called me a Yankee bitch."

"That's not the first time I've heard you mention that 'Yankee bitch' thing. That really riles you, doesn't it?"

"Well, my great-great-grandfather must be cursing me from his grave over it."

70

Ruth smiled and got up, heading toward the sink with the pile of dishes. I got up, too. A thought occurred to me. "Jim, has Lukas been out of the office more than usual lately?"

"Yeah, I'd say he has been."

"Do you think you could nose around and see what he was working on? It could've been his sideline, whatever that is, but you never can tell. People put their papers in strange places sometimes. Something could connect."

Jim nodded. "I can go through his files in the office. No one would think twice about it."

"Good. Okay, now let's call that boy of yours." I dialed the number, and when I got Jesse on the line, I handed the receiver over to his parents and went out to sit in the garden.

When I came in, we agreed on the details of what would happen next. Jim didn't like Eugene's going with us, but could see the necessity for it. I would get them into my rented car and meet Ruth and Greg in northern Virginia tomorrow night. Ruth would go home alone, back to Jim, and I would head west with a car full of boys.

71

NINE

I drove from there straight to the airport. When there was an extra seat on a plane going to Philly I took it. From Philly I got on a flight to Boston.

At Logan someone had made huge sculptures with moving parts that played some hot-stuff modern music. A little ball moved down a chute and ran under hammers that in turn hit little teensy xylophones, which caused percussion instruments to bang joyously. Each movement caused another sound, and precipitated another movement, which caused another sound, and so on. There were two of the sculptures in huge glass cases and at any one moment there were a good fifteen to twenty people standing around, killing time, fascinated. Every so often those people would be replaced by others, and on it went, just like the sculptures inside the case, life and art woven into a fine mesh.

On the flight to Portland, I fell sound asleep. My body ached fiercely and the tiny airplane seats weren't helping all that much. When I woke up I was in winter again. Below me I saw frozen lakes and iced-over evergreens. A snowplow was out cleaning the highway that snaked below. I looked over at my seatmate, a tired-looking soldier. "I hate winter, don't you?"

He shrugged. "Beats where I've been." I didn't ask.

When we landed the sun was starting to set. I made my way over to the car rental section and was given a choice between economy and comfort. I chose comfort, in the form of a Pontiac LeMans, tan-colored to fit in with every other family car on the highway. The open road was calling.

I was starving by the time I got to Freeport, but I wasn't in the mood for the L. L. Bean hysteria that permeates the place. I waited until the Brunswick exit and stopped off at a little joint on the main street that served up great clam rolls and fries. It was that kind of night. I headed out to I-95.

The Pontiac was outfitted with a decent sound system. I put on a tape by some friends who've played music together throughout all the years everyone else has gotten married, had kids, got divorced, gotten bitter. The opening song, "Beaches," was both infinitely sad and hopeful, played with only piano accompaniment. The lyrics washed right over me:

> Out where the light never shines
> she took you there with her voice
> and then left you alone
> oh how your blood did turn cold
> in the quiet of the night
> oh if you could only grow old
> and get away from this fright.

The song went on to turn itself around and tell about all the ways no one was ever really alone. The next song was a more direct commentary on our modern life and times. It had a steady, pulsating reggae beat and told a bit about the dark side of the rainbow:

> Hard times, you'll know 'em if you see 'em
> hard times, I can barely get my rest
> hard times, it's getting hard to deliver
> hard times really put you to the test
> nobody knows where the hard time's coming
> but the hard times.

73

The refrain allowed the backup singers to lend some hope—they ended each line with the words "push 'em back." The last few minutes of the song were filled with percussion and the steadily rising call-and-answer chant of "push 'em back, push 'em back, push 'em back." It made you remember that there was always a chance for the downtrodden to triumph, but it never made triumph seem too easy.

At Augusta I got off the interstate. I stopped at a Dunkin' Donuts and bought a whole-wheat doughnut, which I ate while I waited for a fresh pot of coffee to be brewed. I got back into the car with the coffee and headed up Route 3, going northeast.

It turned out to be slow going. From February to April the roads are filled with something called frost heaves, which are lethal splits in the highway, caused by expanding and contracting ground underneath the roads, or by underground springs, depending on who you talk to. These are usually accompanied by huge dips that threaten to tear out the bottom of your car. As spring nears, potholes join the frost heaves, to add to everyone's misery. Hit a patch of ice while you're braking to soften the effects of a frost heave and just see what happens.

Along the way I passed some interesting place names, which always made me wonder. I hit the turnoff for South China, and shortly afterward Palermo, soon followed by East Palermo. I shook my head. Whenever this happened, I could picture desperate immigrants putting up with untold hardships to arrive at a new land, only to find a spot that's chosen for its familiarity, with an old name thrown on top out of lonesomeness.

Soon, the Pontiac and I hit Belfast, which brought more interesting pictures to mind. I wondered what Belfast, Ireland, really looked like. Belfast, Maine, is where Route 3 meets up with the coastal Route 1, and where I always look forward to getting my first real whiff of the sea.

I followed Route 1 to Bucksport, an old former shipbuilding town whose high green bridge over the Penobscot River made you think of the days when ships did all the hauling to these parts. In those days, I thought, you stayed put in the winter, even more than now. Your horse and wagon took you where you wanted or needed to go. It couldn't have been easy. I shivered. I really was beginning to hate winter.

I showed up at Molly's house in Tillman at ten o'clock. Her lights were on and I could hear the stereo playing softly. It sounded like Chet Baker's trumpet, with maybe Stan Getz. If she was surprised to see me, it didn't show.

"There you are," she said. "I've been wondering about you."

I walked in. "Are they all right?"

"Couldn't be better," she said, "unless they got to go outside, maybe."

"Littlefield?"

"He's okay, too, but then Fred's taking good care of him. Not to worry, he says."

Fred, my upstairs neighbor, was a trucker who had stopped hauling in order to live closer to his elderly mother. He was as nice a guy as you could find, quiet, considerate, and devoted to his little yapping dog, which liked Littlefield a lot more than vice versa. We had this little animal exchange every now and again.

"What happened to you, Lil? You look awful."

"You don't look all that great yourself. Did you get a new haircut?" I grumped.

"Uh huh," she said. "Sit down before you do one of your famous fainting tricks. I'll get the tea water going."

I sighed. It was no use telling anyone anything confidential—they always threw it back in your face later. Molly knew that in fifth grade I'd fainted one day when it was too hot. I'd fallen out of my desk chair. My best friend told me afterward that I'd landed so hard it had shaken the floor. I had internalized that to the point of feeling like a klutz ever since. From now on I was going to keep my own counsel.

Molly handed me a cup of steaming tea. Ah—Lapsang Souchong, my favorite. It felt great going down. I felt myself beginning to forgive her for her thoughtless remark.

"So, Ms. Private Detective, tell me what's what," she said. Molly never paid any attention to my moods.

I told her most of it. When I was finished she looked wide awake, but I was beginning to droop. "So you're gonna take them tomorrow? Eugene too? What's Cooper think about the old man going?"

"Well, he'd rather I didn't have to take him, but I think he's resigned to it. All his attention's on the boy; I kind of slipped Eugene in."

"Lil, don't you want to wait until you're feeling better before you go off to God knows what?"

"Yeah, but I don't see that I have that option. With Lukas roaming around, to stay here any longer would seem like a foolish risk."

I yawned. It had been a long day, one of several.

"Can I use the couch?"

"Look behind you." I turned around. Molly had brought out my favorite quilt and a big, fluffy down pillow. All I had to do was to stretch out.

I took her hand gratefully. "What would I do without you?"

"Don't find out," she said. "I want you to be careful, Lil. Really careful. I know you're tough, but this guy is a stone-cold killer. He won't play fair, you know."

"Neither will I, not with him. I promise you that."

She looked at me long and hard. "Get some sleep. You've got a long day tomorrow."

And a weird one, I thought. Two teenagers and an old man weren't my usual kind of traveling companions, but then maybe the variety would do me some good.

I knocked on Fred's door at six A.M. He answered with a mug of coffee in his hand. It smelled great.

"Lil! You're back. Great—we all missed you." He lowered his voice to a near whisper. "Littlefield might be a little bit mad at you. He wouldn't even eat last night until I offered him some mussels I was fixing for my supper."

"Huh. I'll just bet. That's his oldest trick in the world, Fred. I'm surprised you fell for that one."

Fred grinned. Fred had a nice smile. He put his hand over the side of his mouth to shield the animals from his part of the conversation. "I know it's a trick, because Susan does it too." Susan was his dog, a little piece of fluff with a tail and a tongue.

Speaking of the devil, Susan ran up and stuck her wet nose on my leg, making me flinch. It was her standard greeting. I felt like a human hankie.

Littlefield casually ambled up to me, giving my leg a nonchalant sideswipe. Then he turned his back and started licking himself furiously. I guess he showed me. I scooped him up and covered his little furry face with kisses and coos of love. He rewarded me with a fierce frown and a grunt. Then he jumped down and took a potshot at Susan on his way to the couch. There he settled in for a luxurious cat bath, a real one this time. It meant he was pleased.

Fred poured me a cup of java. It was good coffee, trucker style, meant to deliver a real kick. "How's your case, Lil? Get it all settled?" He tactfully omitted any reference to my bruised face.

"Don't I wish." I hesitated. "Fred, do you think you could look after Littlefield for a bit? It might be a long bit, maybe even a month. I've gotta be out of state for a while."

Fred looked at me intently.

"I don't want to say much more than that it's connected with the case I'm working on. It's turned out to be a major pain in the butt."

He frowned. "Is somebody after you, Lil? Because you can depend on my help, you know."

I did know. Fred was a member of the NRA, a fact that never failed to surprise the hell out of me whenever I thought about it. He had a virtual arsenal upstairs, though I'd never actually seen a gun of his outside the handcrafted oak display case he kept in the living room.

"Thanks, Fred, but I'm going a different way with this one. If you could look after Littlefield and keep an eye on my place, that'd be helping me a lot. But tell me honestly, will Littlefield cramp your style for that long? Because I could get Molly to look after him."

"No, no, no. We like having him here. Susan loves having a friend about while I'm at work. I think she's a little lonely for other animals. And Littlefield always perks us up." He smiled.

77

I smiled back at him. "Perks us up" was a polite way to put it. "I owe you a big one for this, Fred. Someday my ship will come in and I'll give its contents to you."

He laughed. "Let's just wait and see what's on that ship, if you don't mind." I had to admit he had a point.

He left the room to get dressed for work. I stretched out on his couch with Littlefield on my stomach. We stared into each other's eyes until it made Littlefield sleepy. He yawned and I could see all of his sharp little predator's teeth, meant to kill at once. I felt a sudden rush of love for him that made my throat feel tight and swollen. "You take care now, cat. Mama'll be home for you soon."

He stretched out a paw and laid it over my bosom, with his chin on top. For the first time, I was scared to death.

Jesse and Eugene were glad to see me. When I told them my plan, they looked at each other for a meaningful moment, then back at me.

"Dad's gonna let us do this? He's gonna let Greg and Grandfather go, too? Man, I can't believe it." At least Jesse was impressed. Eugene looked more doubtful.

"You sure he knows his old man is going, huh? I can't imagine he'd put up much of a fight about my good health."

I ducked the issue. "Let's not worry too much about details just now. Eugene, Molly's prepared to get someone to close up your trailer until you get back, if that's okay. If either of you needs more clothes, let's just buy them on the way. I want to be on the road in fifteen minutes."

Eugene whistled softly through his teeth. "Your friend said it might be best to prepare for something like this, so I brought a few things with me. The boy, here, doesn't have much, though."

He's got his life, I thought.

I made a couple of quick calls from the phone booth outside the motel. By seven-fifteen we were on the road, with me at the wheel, Jesse in the passenger seat, and Eugene holding down the backseat. In Brewer we gassed up the Pontiac. We stopped one more time in Bangor, to grab a bag of breakfast stuff from a fast-food place.

Then we headed down 95.

78

TEN

By the time we drove around Boston it was beginning to feel a little bit warmer. Near Hartford, Connecticut, a road crew jammed up traffic for a good hour of stop-and-start, which caused some mild to severe swearing in the Pontiac. We finally came to the workmen who had caused the snarl. There were four of them with a hand roller and a couple of shovels. One was sitting down smoking a cigarette. Eugene tapped me on the shoulder. I glanced into the rearview mirror. "You know what?" he said. "If they had five thumbs each they couldn't get one up their ass."

I laughed out loud, something I hadn't done enough of lately. I glanced at Jesse, who was smiling. He'd been quiet for most of the trip, but then he'd had a lot to think about.

We stopped in Brewster, New York, to eat. We'd reached diner country and the food was good—big platters of hot roast-beef sandwiches and coffee. Eugene shed a layer of clothes before getting back into the Pontiac. He was looking pretty good. Maybe being on the road agreed with him; he'd certainly done a lot of traveling in his time. I wondered how much of it he was still able to remember.

The Eastern Seaboard is a long and monotonous stretch of highway that shows off the worst that progress has to offer. If in Maine we take our clean air and water a bit for granted, it's somewhere around the New Jersey Turnpike that I'm reminded of the mortality of the human race and possibly the planet. Smog made the late-afternoon light look hazy, and fumes from the tractor-trailers that dwarfed us made me catch my breath. We stopped for a while at a turnpike rest stop and did just that.

The three of us grabbed Cokes and piled into a booth to watch the action at the hub of the industrial wheel. Eugene whistled to himself again, softly. "Whew! Looks like a swarm of bees, don't it?"

"Killer bees, maybe." Jesse said.

I was surprised. "Jesse, you live in a city. You should be used to this. We're the country hicks here."

"Well, Richmond's different from this. It's kinda slow, I guess." He brightened. "Wanna hear a joke? Okay, how many Richmonders does it take to change a light bulb?"

We didn't know. "Three," he said triumphantly. "One to change the light bulb and two to talk about how much better the old one was."

I had to laugh. That was the Richmond I used to know.

Rush-hour traffic slowed us down when we got back on the turnpike, but we kept moving. After Philly, it cleared out some and we listened to some good big-city radio. Jesse and I liked a lot of the same stuff out of the current rock bag—Sinéad O'Connor, U-2, XTC, UB-40, and several other groups that sounded like names of sports cars. Eugene tended toward country music, which we listened to part of the time, out of politeness. I could see that Jesse didn't like it much, but his parents had raised him so well that his distaste probably wasn't noticeable to Eugene. What we heard sounded like country-music versions of FM and AM radio schlock. Why weren't they playing Emmylou Harris, k. d. lang, Lyle Lovett, Nanci Griffith, and Robert Earl Keen, I wondered.

We lost our daylight. Jesse curled up in the backseat for some shut-eye and Eugene leaned his head against the passenger window and dozed, too. I kept driving. They would have to pry my foot off the accelerator. I love road trips under almost any circumstances.

Driving around Baltimore and D.C. took forever. Traffic had thinned, but what there was drove fast, changed lanes without warning, tailgated and weaved recklessly. I began to think the Pontiac had a target painted on it.

At eleven-thirty I saw the Arlington exit and took it. My eyes were burning with fatigue. I pulled into the Colonial Arms Motel at eleven forty-five and woke up my sleeping companions. Ruth was leaning against the Volvo, smoking a cigarette. She waved to us and then rapped on the window of her car. A boy about Jesse's age blinked tiredly before recognition dawned on his face. Then he smiled broadly and gave us the thumbs-up gesture. My crew, I thought fondly.

So far, so good.

A curious reunion took place. Jesse enveloped his mother in a huge bear hug that lifted her off her feet. Ruth laughed and tousled his hair, which made him toss her around again. The two of them were a nice act to catch—obviously, they were close, and that's something for a teenage boy and his mother. Greg had hung around grinning shyly while this was going on, and now he and Jesse greeted each other with high fives and little punches to the upper arm, followed by backslaps and more punches, this time light ones to the gut. I took this to be the teenage boys' equivalent of bear hugs.

Eugene was the last to get out of the car; it must have been an awkward moment for him. He hung back on the far side of the Pontiac, leaning his arms against the roof, smoking a cigarette, watching. While the boys were still occupied with each other I nodded my head in his direction and whispered to Ruth, "That's Eugene over there."

She stood quietly for the smallest moment. "So that's him," she said in a near whisper. I'd never before taken the time to think what this old man must mean to this woman, who only knew him as a source of her husband's pain. It was another proof of her good character that she walked over to him and coaxed him away from

81

the car. I don't think I was exactly eavesdropping when I heard her say to him, "Eugene, I'm Ruth, and I've been wanting to meet you for a long time." The old man looked like putty in her hands.

Now that we'd made it here, my legs felt like rubber and my body ached all over. I needed a three-day sleep. I looked around for a good place to collapse. That not being possible, I did the next best thing, which was to take up Ruth's old position by the Volvo. "Hey, Jess," I said, "who's your pal? I thought you said Greg was coming."

"Oh, sorry. Where are my manners? Lil, I'd like you to meet my friend Greg. Greg, this is Lil. She's a private detective."

Greg looked at Ruth with surprise. "Is she really? You didn't tell me that."

Ruth nodded. "I thought Jesse could tell you."

Greg looked back at me. "You don't look much like Magnum, P.I."

"We're different types," I said. "I'm a lot better-looking." I stuck out my hand for a shake.

Greg was a cute redhead with freckles. Where Jesse was long and lean, Greg was shorter and beefier, part fat and part muscle. I would've said his face belonged to a boy younger than somewhere between sixteen and seventeen. In a flash, I could see him as the perpetual younger brother, a role he probably fell into naturally, both out of need and out of habit by now. I wondered if that was the basis of the boys' relationship. Growing up without parents or siblings must have left holes hard to fill.

"Thanks for letting me go along, Lil. I can help you with the driving if you need it." He eyed the Pontiac.

"Well, I suppose it could come to that."

Jesse laughed first, and when Greg realized I'd been joking with him he shook his head sheepishly. "He's always trying to get hold of a steering wheel," Jesse said. "We had driver's ed, but we don't get to practice."

Teenage boys, by and large, aren't my favorite drivers. When I was growing up in Virginia, a carload of them used to get killed every few years, drag racing down curvy roads. "Thanks, guys. I guess we'll see how it goes."

Ruth and Eugene joined us around the Volvo. "I don't know about anyone else, but I'm dead on my feet," I said. We looked like a pretty tired lot, now that I noticed it.

I looked at Ruth. "It's too late to be driving back to Richmond, isn't it? Wouldn't you rather share a room with me?"

Ruth nodded. "In fact, I already got us some rooms. Eugene, I got you a single so you could get some peace and quiet. I put the boys together. Lil, I didn't think you'd mind if I got us a double."

It suited me fine. She started taking things out of the car.

Eugene eyed Greg. "Boy, it's good to see you standin' here fit as a fiddle. Jesse was some worried about you."

Greg smiled politely at the old man. I was wondering if he had known anyone at all like Eugene, and my guess would've been no. He seemed awkward, as if he didn't know the social rules for this interaction.

I decided to help Eugene out. "I've brought Eugene here along to help keep an eye out for you guys. I thought a traveling man might come in handy."

Greg gratefully took the cue. "You like to travel?"

"Boy, I've been hoboing around since before you were born. I've been damned near everywhere you can get to from here." Eugene's chest swelled a bit, in admiration of his own story.

Greg looked at Jesse for corroboration. Jesse nodded. "He's pretty cool, man. He used to ride the rails."

Greg's eyes widened a bit in surprise. He looked at Eugene again, and I suspected he saw a different person this time. "I'd like to hear about that. I only know about it from movies."

Eugene nodded wisely. "Yeah, most good things in this country have been taken away from us, you know."

I broke in, too tired to stand there and listen to the story Eugene was getting ready to tell. "You boys had better get some good sleep tonight. We're driving straight through, and it can take all the sap out of you."

Ruth dug the room keys out of her jeans, along with a handful of change for sodas. We walked the boys to their room and showed Eugene his, which was right next door. Ours was across the little courtyard.

I flopped down on the first bed I saw. Ruth pulled a bottle out of her bag and held it toward me. "I thought we might need a snort." It was George Dickel, king of bourbons. Ah, sometimes ecstasy comes when we least expect it. "How did you get to be so perfect?" I asked gratefully.

She flopped down on the other end of the bed and kicked off her shoes. "Would you settle for 'born that way'?"

I would. Things were definitely looking up.

The smell of coffee woke me. For a few seconds I couldn't recall where I was, but I knew I'd been in worse places. I opened an eye. Sunlight streamed in through the window, along with a warm breeze. Ah, yes, the Southland. Ruth sat on a chair in front of the vanity table, running a comb through her hair.

I lay there quietly, watching her for a few moments, waiting for my heart to somehow right itself, to come back to its old familiar beat.

Then Ruth glanced back through the mirror, and smiled.

"Morning, Lil."

Right then and there, I gave myself a stern talking-to. This was a client, a straight, married woman. We both had our jobs to do.

"I thought you were gonna have coiffed hair," I said.

She laughed. "Forget that. I'm definitely not the coiffed type."

"How do you stand those country-club dances?" Suddenly I found there were lots of things I was wondering about.

"Well, for one thing we don't go all that often—the only one we can be counted on to show up for is the Christmas dance. That one's fun; everyone's all dressed up and the Charlottesville Swing Orchestra usually plays. They have a woman singer I particularly like. I can close my eyes and be somewhere else, even pretend I'm dancing to Ellington himself." She stared into the mirror, dreamily.

"So the country club isn't your kind of thing, then." I knew I was probing, but damn it, I wanted to know.

"Well, I admit to using the pool quite regularly, but I sure don't live there like some of the members." She eyed me through the mirror. "Are we a bit of a snob, perhaps?"

I flushed. "Well, let's just say I grew up in a different Virginia, and I'm curious about you more affluent types."

She laughed again, and the moment's tension evaporated. "Lil, I grew up on a farm down in the Tidewater. Peanuts and tobacco. Jim—well, you know his story in part, I suppose—his father a drunk, his mother working in the silk mill in Orange in order to raise her kids and get away from Eugene. We don't exactly have country-club beginnings; it's just that Jim's done so well with his business that people let our backgrounds slide. This is still Virginia, though; we know no one's actually forgotten where we came from. Oh, no." She shook her head and smiled. "That would be too much to ask."

I wondered briefly if anything was ever the way it seemed.

"Here," she said. "I got us some coffee."

I sat up. "Where'd you get coffee?"

"Believe me, I could find coffee after a nuclear attack. I've got a sixth sense. I also noticed a Dunkin' Donuts down the street last night. It's not cappuccino, but it's not bad."

"That sounds like one of those awful country songs you hear on the radio these days, written by some country singer from New Jersey." I sipped my coffee gratefully. "Was that a pool I saw last night, or was I hallucinating?"

"It was, and I've already tried it out. It's not bad, small but clean. Want a dip before breakfast? I told the boys we could have breakfast together in a half-hour or so, so there's time."

I tried stretching a bit, sitting on the side of the bed, then standing and doing some slow, deep yoga movements. My body protested at first, then started to relax. A swim would complete the workout and finish waking me up. I gathered up my things.

"Thanks for the coffee, Ruth. And for, uh, last night. It was good having company." I paused at the door.

She shrugged, a little smile playing on her lips.

"Any time," she said.

I hit the pool. Afterward, I stood under as hot a shower as I could manage, and let the water massage away some of the bodily hurt. Toweling off, I stood naked in front of the full-length mirror. I saw an older version of the person I'd always been. Always a tall child, I'd grown into a moderately tall woman, standing five eight, with good muscles on my big-boned frame.

I was in pretty good shape, the result of a lot of years of swimming and yoga. I'd always liked my arms and legs for their solidity. They made me feel capable. I knew I moved well without a lot of thought going into it. Swimming had formed my shoulders, made them strong. I was secretly proud of my breasts: They made me look good in a sweater.

Last summer's tan had faded; I needed some sun.

I checked my brown hair, found a little bit of gray starting to replace the area that had been perpetually sun-bleached when I lived in the South. I had my father's thick eyebrows and lashes, and my mother's hazel eyes. And whose eyes are not serious in a mirror? I examined the little hints of wrinkles—some would call them laugh lines—and thought: not bad for a broad pushing forty.

Basically, I didn't give a damn about these small signs, an attitude I showed at the slightest provocation. I knew the cost in experience of each gray hair and every minute crease of the skin: signs of a life fully lived. The dream of eternal youth couldn't compete with that.

I've been told I have an intelligent look about me, but I've never been able to detect that. All I can ever see is the child underneath, still living with this changing body in an easy partnership.

"Not bad, old girl." A compliment never hurts.

I threw on some traveling clothes—old jeans, a faded T-shirt that said 1983 AUSTIN CHRONICLE MUSIC POLL AWARDS CEREMONY, a light-blue denim shirt on top of that, and sneakers with no socks. For now, I packed my Walther into the leather bag that would go wherever I went. I didn't see any need to start wearing my shoulder holster yet.

Before heading over to the boys' room, where Ruth was waiting for me, I went outside to a phone booth I'd spotted the night before. I didn't want any record of this call showing up where it shouldn't. It rang five times before a breathless voice picked it up. "Mom, it's me. I'm at a pay phone, so this'll have to be short."

My mother was a renowned conversationalist. "Why, Lil, honey, where are you, girl?"

"I'm in northern Virginia, heading west with some clients, but you don't know that, okay?"

"If you say so, then I don't. Is everything okay, though? You're all right, aren't you, Lil?"

"Yeah, Mom, I'm fine. I'm working on a case that has a Virginia connection, so I've been having a hard time not trying to sneak in a visit, that's all."

"Well, for heaven's sake, don't fight it so. Just get on down here and I'll fry you some chicken. I'll even cook some string beans and potatoes together in the pressure cooker, the way you like 'em. Bring your clients along. You know I don't mind meeting new people—I never have, yet."

She'd do it, too. My mouth watered. My mother's fried chicken was nothing to mess around with; I'd watched her make it, I'd even used cast-iron pans that had been in the family, but still I couldn't begin to reproduce the taste. I sighed. "I can't, Mom. No one on this case knows anything about you, and for safety reasons I wanna keep it that way. Okay?"

"Well, it's sweet you always want to protect me so, but what on earth would you do if you were a detective in the state of Virginia? You couldn't keep your relatives such a secret then."

"Oh yes I could. I'd make you change your names and move to Iowa. Put a guard on you and never let you go outside. I'd have to work the kinks out, but it'd go something like that."

She laughed her good, musical laugh. "I'm just wondering if we made a mistake in giving you that Roy Rogers gun and holster set that time."

The operator interrupted to say that I would have to deposit more money or hang up. "Mom, I'd better go, but don't worry, I'm fine. I'll call you again when I know what's what."

"Make sure you do, honey. I love you." The connection was cut off before I could respond.

I collected Ruth, Eugene, and the boys, and we headed off to breakfast in the motel dining room. Normally I won't get near a motel restaurant except in Louisiana, but time was of the essence and we needed to get going. We all ordered big breakfasts. Eugene's cigarette was stinking up the works, but the old man looked happy so I wasn't about to spoil his mood. Ruth was solicitous of him and very respectful. I didn't know if Eugene was going to have a son or not, but he definitely already had a daughter-in-law and a grandson. I watched him soaking up the attention like a sponge.

A glance at the wall clock behind the cash register told me it was eight. I studied the boys. They looked sleepy enough to have talked through much of the night, but also gave off a sense of excitement mixed with a good dollop of plain old fear of the unknown. I couldn't much blame them.

I caught Ruth giving Jesse a worried look, but I gave her credit for not letting him see it. The woman's only child was in danger, and she was entrusting me with his safety.

It was at times like this that I often wondered what it would've been like to have stayed in music for my livelihood. A nice, steady, Holiday Inn gig seemed like heaven to me right now, but that very thought had been one of the things that had run me out of music. "Grow up, Lillian," I said to myself, "and get this show on the road."

When we'd finished eating, Ruth looked over at me. "It's time, isn't it?"

I pushed my chair back. "Yeah, I guess it is."

Jesse spoke up. "Mom, why don't you come with us? Dad can cook okay." Jesse was having a hard time pulling away from Ruth, too.

Ruth smiled at her son and squeezed his hand. "Thanks, honey, but I don't guess I'd better leave your dad alone just now. He's pretty upset, you know."

Jesse lowered his head. "Yeah, I know."

After paying the bill, Ruth joined the rest of us outside. She gave her son a long hug. "Just remember your dad loves you very much. What's happening has nothing to do with that. He'll want to talk to you about this whole thing when it's over, so don't feel that any of it's your fault. Will you promise me this?"

The boy mumbled something and nodded.

"Do what Lil tells you, now. She knows what she's doing—she's a professional. Then when everything's okay again, we'll have a welcome-home party for you boys, and Lil too, that'll knock the socks off the old fuddy-duddies across the street."

We piled our things into the car. Jesse and Greg settled into the back and Eugene sat up front in the navigator's seat. He had his window down, and Ruth put her hand lightly on his arm. "Don't be a stranger now, Eugene. I can see we'll be friends." She leaned over and kissed him on the cheek. Eugene beamed.

I finished arranging stuff in the trunk and slammed down the lid.

I turned around and Ruth treated me to a good-bye hug. Then she looked me in the eye and said in a low voice, "You can handle this, right?"

I returned her look. "I'll give it everything I've got." It didn't seem like enough, but what more was there?

She nodded. You don't have to explain reality to people who've put in time on a farm.

"Keep a low profile for a few days, and be extra careful. Don't go places by yourself at night, stuff like that. Just to be safe." She nodded again, a little solemnly this time.

I got into the driver's seat. My crew looked only a little more apprehensive than I felt myself.

Looking back at Ruth one last time, I said: "You've been a rock. Thanks."

"Sure, Lil. And call us when you need more money. We'll wire whatever you need."

Then wire me some guts, I thought.

We headed off for the wild blue yonder.

We drove for the next thirty-six hours.

That first morning we enjoyed the drive through Virginia and the sweetness of its early spring. The Shenandoah Valley was starting to come awake after its winter hibernation. I thought of what would already be growing there this time of year: the skunk cabbage with its own glowing light bulb inside for channeling sunlight;

wild ginger, that great favorite of slugs; mayapples; hepatica, also known as liverwort for its beneficial medicinal uses; the glorious tulip magnolia, which my family called tulip poplar—one of the first all-out wildly blooming treats of early spring. Jonquils would have been sticking up out of the late winter–early spring snows, trying to bloom before anything else. Usually they made it by Easter, along with the lilies of the valley, my grandfather's favorite flower. Next would come yellow bells, which were really forsythia, and bluebells, or Mertensia. After that would come the beautiful lilacs, dogwoods, sweet-smelling magnolias, azaleas, and tulips that make Virginia among the prettiest places in the world in the spring. I fought an overwhelming desire to cancel the whole damned trip and go nestle in the warm glow of family, friends, and familiarity. But I just kept on driving.

Tennessee is always disconcerting to me. For some of the time, we drove through old farmland and quiet, green parts of the Smoky Mountains, where nothing much had changed, to the naked eye at least, for many a year. Then we hit the stretch of highway between Knoxville and Nashville where huge stinking trucks threaten to swallow you whole and then puke you back out. I felt bad-tempered and vile through most of that stretch. After that, there was a decent bit of highway before Memphis, which was always a landmark of sorts: Besides being the home of Elvis, it was where you had to cross the Mississippi River to get to the West. After the bridge there you suddenly found yourself in the flat delta land of Arkansas. We saw hawks on what seemed like every telephone wire and fencepost we passed. They looked out at us, impassively.

Day passed into night and back into daylight. Everything blended together: the road, the car, my traveling companions, the music on the radio. I did the lion's share of the driving, which is my preference, but reluctantly turned the wheel over to each boy once when I started to see double. Eugene claimed not to drive.

We ate barbecue, tacos, burgers, and pie, accompanied by lots of coffee. Somewhere in Arkansas we began to come across my all-time favorite truckstop, the 76. By this time things were starting to get a little fuzzy around the edges, but one event that impressed me, at least, was a 76 breakfast of country ham, redeye gravy, grits, and biscuits, served to us by a waitress with more than a hundred different trucker's emblems sewn to her denim jacket. She was slim-hipped, tanned, and a little gnarled, but so warm of spirit we almost stayed right there with her. One look told her story: She had seen a little bit of everything life could dish out and still had the guts and the desire to keep on going.

Sleep deprivation makes me crazy. After a while, conversation dropped by the wayside; we were all exhausted beyond words. Music kept us going. I had brought a case that held 120 cassettes and during the day and a half it took to get from Virginia to Texas we listened to almost every one of them: Van Morrison, Miles Davis, Emmylou Harris, Peggy Lee, Sheila Jordan—lots of Sheila—John Coltrane, Patti Smith, Louis Armstrong, old Byrds, Dylan (I seemed to have listened to "Sad-Eyed Lady of the Lowlands" twice), the Cowboy Junkies, the Stones, B. B. King, Bonnie Raitt, you name it, we heard it. It was our lifeline. Every now and then Eugene would ask me who someone was, but if he had any particular musical prejudices he didn't show them to me. Sometimes I'd glance over and he'd be looking straight ahead, smoking, tapping out the beat gently on the side of the car. He was quiet and self-contained and I had the distinct feeling he was having the time of his life. Every now and then he'd point at something and say "nice" or "pretty" or "awful" and usually he was right on the mark.

During one long stretch when the boys were asleep Eugene told me a little about his life: how he was raised in the rolling hills of central Virginia on his father's farm, and how first his mother, then his father, had succumbed to influenza during a hard winter when he was still in his teens. He'd tried farming alone, and for a while he'd done okay, but soon his loneliness and grief had sent him scurrying to the store for liquor. He'd met Frances, a young woman from nearby Orange, at a dance, and she'd been charmed by his awkward way of dancing and his attempts to be dashing. After they married, he worked the farm with the help of Frances. When he failed to display a knack for running the place, his wife, he thought, lost respect for him.

By now, Eugene and Frances had a daughter, Anne, who loved her father enough to make up for his wife's increasing lack of interest. Frances had finally gotten a job in the silk mill in Orange, and managed to save the farm single-handedly. This had driven Eugene into a depression that was only relieved by more drinking. Frances became pregnant again, and this time the baby was a boy, whom they named James after Eugene's father. But his wife had had enough; she moved to an apartment in Orange with her children. For a while, she visited on weekends so that the kids could be with their father, but as Eugene sank lower she eventually stopped the visits. She sold the farm to get back what money she could, with the stipulation that Eugene be allowed to remain on the property as a hired hand, living in one of the outbuildings. That was the best she could do under the circumstances, Eugene said, but it finished him off. He left the county in shame and woke up a lot of years later.

The boys, when they weren't writhing around in the backseat trying to find a comfortable spot to sleep, were a little wide-eyed. Sure, they'd chatter, as teenagers will, but I could feel their intimidation just the same; this was a long way away from their prep-school existence. Here the world consisted of road and more road; an occasional stop to pee or eat was the only relief from the monotonous hum of the engine. The boys were game, though, and tried their best not to jump out of their skins. I, for one, appreciated it. It left me free to switch into my automatic-pilot mode, which would get us into the state of Texas the fastest. About thirty miles from the Arkansas-Texas border we passed a highway sign for a place called Hope, and we made much of that for the next few miles.

At Texarkana we shrieked for joy and blew the car horn at everything that passed us. We were finally in Texas. I chuckled to myself and the guys asked me what was so funny. I then told them of the worst motel stay of my life, in Texarkana with my old band. The place was called the Torch and it was so filthy we'd tossed a coin to see who had to sleep on the bed. The morning after had revealed a swimming pool green with algae and rot. A Chicano family of ten or twelve mirrored my own misery as they poured out of their sweltering room into the sweltering heat outside. That had been my first introduction to Texas in the late sixties, and I had almost fled.

I had, in fact, fled Texas a couple of times, but something always kept me coming back. The heat nearly kills me and there's a wildness in the air that is both exhilarating and terrifying. I even have a weird affection for the places in Texas no one's supposed to like at all, like Lubbock and other points west. There's something steady and timeless in the unending miles of cotton, cattle, and oil fields of west Texas. At the same time as I'm struggling for breath in the relentless heat, there's a joyousness in my heart that threatens to come out of my mouth in the form of a scream, or a war whoop.

We swallowed up the miles, one by one. The Pontiac did what it was designed to do: give a comfortable, reliable ride.

At Dallas I think we all experienced lurching stomachs at the hugeness of the city and the imposing gold skyscrapers profiled against the horizon. There we connected up with I-35 and I pointed out places I'd known personally.

In Waco I showed my riders a place—now a spa—where my band had played for a miserable rainy weekend. We'd been promised living quarters for our three-day gig, only to discover the club owners intended for us to stay in a leaky basement with wet mattresses on the floor and a toilet in the corner, without benefit of door or curtain. There had been an incident with a scorpion in a sleeping bag. I now reported these events joyfully: We were nearing Austin, the home of my heart.

We sneaked into town on I-35. I excitedly identified landmarks on the horizon: The U.T. tower, where Charles Whitmore had seen fit to shoot every passerby he could. The rolling hills of LBJ's beloved hill country now come all the way into town, giving it a friendly green flavor. The Colorado River runs through the city, bringing relief from the muggy heat that lasts about the same length of time as Maine spends trapped in the icy arms of winter.

We couldn't see all of this from the interstate, but I couldn't stop talking all of a sudden. I took the Martin Luther King exit, a name that had raised a few eyebrows when it replaced the old one, Nineteenth Street. From there we drove slowly, with the windows down, taking in the scents of an East Austin spring, which is never all that far from a full-blown summer.

At Chicon I parked the car and we all got out to stretch. Eugene looked around in surprise and said, "Where in the hell are we?" I pointed out a sign over an inconspicuous little shack with BAR-B-Q written in colorful letters on a side window. Where we were was in front of the best barbecue joint in Austin, for my money.

I walked in and a black man pushing sixty who was stirring a big pot of greens looked up with just passing interest at first, and then in surprise. Then he smiled a smile that was so sweet I almost cried.

"Girl, where on earth have you been?" he said. "Come on over here and let me give you a hug."

I was home.

ELEVEN

The boys wolfed down their food before going into the next room to shoot some pool. The place wasn't open yet, so we had it all to ourselves. Eugene and I took longer to eat. But Robert had tales to tell; we needed some catch-up time. Eugene seemed to sense this after a bit, and pushed his chair back from the table.

"That was some mighty good eatin'," he said, "but I think I'd better show those boys how the game is really played." He got up and glanced in at them. "Minnesota Fats, they ain't," he said sorrowfully. "This here's gonna take a little doing." Robert and I were alone.

We chatted for a little while about this and that. I asked him about his wife, Ellie, and their children. By now he had enough grandchildren to form a Little League team. We talked about Austin—how it had and had not changed in the years I'd been gone. He had a wealth of information about the city. Except for a brief stint in the service, he'd spent his entire life there and usually knew what was going down before it actually happened. He'd had his business for thirty years, and during a good many of them he'd featured live bands out back. More than a few fresh young groups had perfected their music, playing night after night under Robert's live oaks, until their sound jelled and other clubs started to get in touch. That was what had brought Robert and me together.

The conversation started to slow down. He gave me a serious look and said, quietly, "Lil, honey, how are you doing? Girl, we didn't know where you were or what had happened to you for a long time. Then I told Ellie, 'If she wanted to be in touch she'd let me know it,' and that's just been the way it's been." He stopped talking then and I could see the hurt in his eyes. "Christmas cards aren't enough—not to your real friends, Lilly."

Robert was the only person besides my mother who ever called me that.

I stared down at the table, fighting back tears, unprepared for the flood of emotion that welled up in me now. But unresolved issues come back, and in a flash I lost seventeen years.

Pride can be an awful thing. In those days Austin was one of the most promising spots in the music world, just starting to come into its own. The music industry had started to hear about all the good groups way down in Austin, Texas, and a couple of local bands had been snapped up with promises of fortune and fame in Los Angeles or New York. I had been riding the wave as hard as anyone, with all my heart. There were deals in the works. Two guys—not one, but two—from L.A. were in touch about possible recording contracts. The band was cooking. Apparently we could do no wrong.

And then Ron got killed—Ron, my soul mate, my band mate since I was a kid. Suddenly it was all over for me. I was accused of his murder, and the town closed ranks so fast I didn't know what had happened to me. Just thinking about it now, I felt waves of grief rising to the surface; they had been lying in wait in the darkness for a long time. I'd had no choice but to try and clear my name. I certainly didn't plan on doing time in the Texas penal system and coming out of it any better than a wild animal that had been caught in a trap. I couldn't have stood it. I'd have gone nuts.

Wilkie, the sleazebag, was behind it; I could just feel it. Him and his purple Lotus. He'd made my skin crawl from the first night he hung around the One Note. He was gonna do this for us, he was gonna do that. The second time he came over to the band house he'd brought some Mexican brown and enough syringes for us all. I'd come walking in as he was tying the tourniquet on Ron's arm. I walked back out the door without saying one word.

After that, Ron was never the same. He started not giving a shit, which certainly wasn't the Ron I knew. He stopped writing the tunes and he stopped talking to me, something he'd done as easily as breathing just weeks before. Wilkie was around a lot, in his awful clothes, with his slicked-back blond hair. He repulsed me; I knew instinctively he was capable of doing anything. I could feel it. But Ron wouldn't listen. Maybe he couldn't.

The night the cops found his body, the first thing I'd thought was "Why would anyone bother to shoot Ron? Just wait another month or so and he'll overdose all by himself." It was an awful thought then, and the years hadn't made it any more palatable.

Then the cops, acting on a tip, searched my room for the gun that had killed him. Wilkie had made the call, of course, after first hiding the pistol in the back of my amp. It was the easiest thing in the world, probably. Even without my prints on the gun, it tested out as the weapon that had shot Ron, and no one listened to me very much after that, though I had three witnesses to say they'd seen me in San Antonio at the crucial time. But a couple of Wilkie's pals were willing to swear they'd seen me in Austin at the time of the murder. The papers had taken it from there. It must have made great copy: "THE ROCK AND ROLL MURDER." After that, my music career was shot. I might as well have lived in the middle of Wyoming as in Austin, Texas, home of the electric guitar.

I'd cleared myself eventually. The cops, though fully prepared to accept me as Ron's killer, hadn't been able to find any motive. There hadn't been one, and no amount of digging had come up with one. But when, on my suggestion, they looked hard at Wilkie, he didn't hold up well at all. They tore up the Lotus when I'd told them I was sure it was where he kept the heroin and God only knew what else. They'd found records of Ron's debt to him, and—after a long night in police custody without his drugs—they got a confession, too. He hadn't done it for what Ron had owed him, he'd done it because it pleased him at the moment. I knew he was still doing hard time in Huntsville and wasn't likely to see the light of day in this lifetime.

And that was where pride had tripped me up. The guys from L.A. had stopped coming, and the bigger clubs were embarrassed to use me—once accused, forever convicted in some people's eyes. I played two miserable gigs in a third-rate beer garden and after the second night I went home and packed up my car. I'd driven all night and ended up in New Mexico before I knew it. The desert felt good after that. It was clean.

I told Robert some of the parts that led up to my life now. "How you been making your living? Still picking that guitar?"

"Not for money, Robert. When I connected Wilkie to the gun, I found something else I was good at. I suppose I have him to thank for that. In New Mexico I apprenticed with a P.I. who was about to retire. He taught me all he knew, which was plenty. I find people who're missing, usually. Other times I solve crimes the police have given up on or aren't too interested in, for one reason or another."

He shook his head. "Well, it's a crying shame you're not playing music, honey. You were damned good."

I smiled at that. "I play all the time, really. I just don't depend on it for my money. You might just say I play for myself, is all."

He thought about that for a minute or two, until he could accept the state of my affairs for now. It was one of the things I'd always admired about Robert. He could flow.

"So who're these people in my pool room? Something tells me they're not your buddies and not your relatives."

And I told him the whole story. "Now I need some help, Robert. I know I didn't accept any from you when the shit hit the fan before, but I could use it now, if you could find it in your heart to forgive me for running out on my friends. Not that it's any real excuse, but I was younger then, and my heart was broken, you know."

"That much I do know, Lilly." He took my hand. His was warm and callused from hard work and too many dishes.

I felt a lump in my throat again. "It's like this, Robert. Austin used to be my town. I think maybe it could be again, if only for a short while. Whatcha think?"

He sat in silence again for a few seconds. I could almost see the wheels turning. Finally he spoke.

"I think you came to the right place."

Robert went in and hung around with Eugene and the boys while I made a couple of calls from the phone in the back room. I was pleased to see he hadn't changed his posters in seventeen years; Buddy Guy, Johnny Copeland, and Clarence "Gatemouth" Brown still shared space with Janis Joplin, the 13th Floor Elevators, and some of the other old hippie bands of the late sixties.

When I'd finished I stood in the doorway of the pool room and nodded to Robert. He had a few calls to make himself. In thirty minutes we were back on the road, this time following Robert's green Cutlass. We stopped twice, once to fill up at a gas station, the second time to buy a few bags of groceries. It was time to get the boys out of sight.

We headed southwest. I usually loved the Texas countryside, but by this time my eyes were burning with fatigue and my brain was on overload. We turned off 290 onto Route 12, headed south. From there we connected up with an old farm-to-market road that was as familiar to me as my own daydreams. Finally we stopped at a little settlement tucked back into some trees.

"Now where are we?" Jesse asked from the backseat in an uncharacteristically whiney voice. "Aren't we gonna stay in a motel, or someplace with a pool? It's too hot."

I tried to fight back irritation. "Try not to judge too fast, Jesse. I realize this is a lot different from what you're used to, but these people are willing to put themselves out for three people they've never met. You might not appreciate this fully now, but you will later."

He shrugged and mumbled something about the heat.

"Believe me, it's not even hot yet! I'm deathly afraid of snakes, but in the middle of the summer I'd just as soon swim in the river out back with the water moccasins as not. I can show you the path later if you'd like."

I turned around before he could see my smile of satisfaction. My mean streak was showing, something that happens when I get too tired.

We sat there in silence after that, while Robert went inside to talk in private first. We'd decided that would be best. I looked around.

The main house was a simple, clapboard, one-story deal that could've used a good coat of fresh paint. But flowers were growing in window boxes in front and the pecan tree that shaded the whole house looked full of promise. There was a sturdy-looking swing on the porch that most likely saw a lot of service during the hell-heat of the summer months. A large live-oak with the remains of a treehouse in its thick, spread-out limbs shaded the side yard. Builders today would've cleared the lot with a bulldozer and then planted puny shrubs that wouldn't have shaded a gnat. Another great example of the white man's progress on our formerly green planet, I thought.

At the back sat a vintage trailer and a tiny little house covered with limestone, something there was no dearth of in these parts. Altogether, the homestead looked neat and cool—Texas neat and Texas cool, not like the Eastern style of groomed and pruned landscapes I had grown up with. The surroundings suggested that the owners of this place would stop doing chores and go fishing at the drop of a hat if the fish were really biting. Judging by the ashes in the round pit in the side yard, they'd already had a fish fry or two this spring. No, this wasn't the Ritz, and I for one was more than glad it wasn't.

I got out to stretch and then leaned against the car, for a little variety. I looked over at Eugene, who had his head back on the seat with his hat over his eyes, cowboy style. The boys were slumped down in the backseat with their legs twisted and folded this way and that. I'd have to try and be patient; nothing in their lives had prepared them to be in this place, at this moment.

I heard a burst of laughter and the screen door swung open. Robert came out, accompanied by his closest friend, a handsome man somewhere between Robert's age and mine. He had the dramatic-looking mustache of the majority of the Spanish-American males in the Southwest. His friendship with Robert had been a pleasant surprise to me years ago; the two minorities had traditionally been at odds more times than not, locally. They'd both been treated badly by the people who considered themselves the "real" Texans, and who still kept the blacks and Chicanos busy scrambling for a place on the lower rungs of the economic ladder, when they could get away with it. This had, of course, often resulted in the kind of hard feelings that emerge when the pecking order has done the job it was intended to do. It spoke well for the two men that their friendship had endured this strongly, and for this long. God knows, it couldn't have been simple or easy.

Joe Portillo was as good-looking as ever. His hair and mustache were still black, but the little laugh lines around his eyes betrayed his age. He still looked fit enough to get the better of a younger man in a fight. Right now his eyes were twinkling, and I knew him well enough to know my presence wasn't the only reason. Joe dearly loved a challenge.

"My goodness, if it isn't our guitar mama! Man, we thought you'd dropped off the face of the earth." He spoke in the lilting accent that I'd missed. "Lena's gonna kill you for beating her here; she's gone to the store." He put a friendly arm around my shoulder and squeezed. "I think she's preparing a feast for you." He gave me a mischievous look. "You haven't forgotten about carne guisada and tortillas, have you? And good salsa, hot enough to take off the top of your head? And frijoles—how could I forget the frijoles? Uhm-um!" He rubbed his belly.

I gave him a hug. I'd missed this wild man.

He continued his little show for the boys' benefit. "Man, I see you brought your kids with you." He peered inside the car. "Come on out—I won't shoot you right away. At least not until we've fed you."

Jesse and Greg smiled shyly, but I could see they were interested. Nobody could resist Joe when he was rolling. He looked at Eugene, then back at me. "I also see you brought us another goat roper."

I shook my head. "Goat roper" was a friendly enough insult,

101

used freely in modern Texas, although I was sure that used in the cattle country of the 1800s it would've meant the start of a fight, with or without six-guns. Joe offered Eugene his hand and said, "You look like you need a beer, partner."

Eugene did, at that. "Well, I guess I do, but I reckon I won't. If I get started, I'll drink you right out of house and home."

Joe took the hint. "Well, that don't matter none. Lena makes her iced tea so strong it'll suit the same purpose, my friend. Come on in."

Lena arrived a few minutes later. She came running toward me with her arms wide open. "Lillian, mi amiga, it's really you." I could feel something start to melt inside me. We hugged long and hard.

Lena was looking good. Age was wearing well on her, as it was on Joe. She still looked like the Aztec goddess I'd remembered, smallish in height but powerful in bearing, and fierce-looking when she wasn't smiling her radiant smile. She was a little plumper than she'd been, but the extra pounds suited her, I thought. She and I had worked together when I'd first moved to Austin, before the band had been able to earn its own living. We'd slung hash in an all-night pancake house that served a mixture of latter-day cowboys, drunks, and hippies with ravenous appetites. We'd spent a lot of our time together in the kitchen plotting our escape, and on the day Lena finally got fired I tore off my filthy apron and ran out the door behind her, laughing. We danced around the parking lot like a couple of idiots, until we finally decided to celebrate with cold margaritas. Three hours and several margaritas later, we called Joe, who gently suggested we leave our cars in the lot and wait for him to pick us up. It was Lena who later introduced me to Robert, who in turn took the band under his protective wing for as long as necessary. She and I had been a good team then, and nothing felt any different with the passage of time.

We spent the rest of the afternoon catching up with each other's lives. It didn't take long for Jesse and Greg to start feeling at home, in spite of the cultural differences. Soon they were watching TV in the back bedroom. Eugene seemed content to listen to the old stories we told; he was quiet, but very much there. Once again it occurred to me that the old man had been out of the mainstream of humanity for a long time. Just maybe, he was enjoying being back.

After dinner—indeed a feast—Lena noticed that the boys were starting to fade. "You hombres had better get to bed, don't you think? You can have that back room with the TV so you won't be too far from the refrigerator."

The boys weren't too sure how to handle this remark, until Lena laughed and slapped each of them lightly on the knee. "Don't take my jokes to heart, fellas; just relax and feel right at home. We've had a houseful of kids, and a couple more polite ones like you won't cramp our style a bit."

They admitted to being sleepy and headed off to bed. I was sure they would be asleep before they had their clothes off.

Eugene was given the trailer out back. Lena had bought it originally for her elderly aunt, who had since died. The little house was saved for me. I would be able to come and go more discreetly, and keep watch if necessary. I knew the boys were inside the main house so that they'd be safe regardless of what happened.

Lena walked me out to the little house. She paused just inside the door, looking around. "You know, my great-great-grandfather built this when he came up from Mexico way back there. He said the thick limestone would keep it cool, and he was right. He'd seen some of those German 'Sunday' houses in Fredericksburg on the way—you know, those tiny little houses the farmers built in town so they could shop on Saturdays and stay over for church."

I nodded. The houses were little charmers, all right. But something was bothering me.

"Lena, I have to get something off my mind."

She made a motion meant to silence me, but I continued. "I'm so grateful that you and Joe are willing to help. Robert was sure it would be okay or I wouldn't have placed you in jeopardy for all the world. You know how much I value your friendship, yours and Joe's."

"Shhh," she said. "None of this is necessary between compadres. My Jose can take care of ten men like this Lukas, my friend, and, besides, I've got a feeling you could probably do this by yourself if you needed to."

I wasn't so sure of that.

We sat down on the bed, allowing a moment's silence to reverberate through the little house. Suddenly Lena laughed. "Remember that guy who used to come in the restaurant about two in the morning, drunk, and order a couple of big breakfasts and give the waitresses shit? You know—dirty blond hair and the fringe jacket?"

I remembered. "Don't tell me he's still out there somewhere in that jacket. No god could be that cruel."

"Maybe not, but I've long suspected God of having a sense of humor. That guy's on the City Council. Made a fortune in computers, or so he says, and lives out by the lake somewhere—a regular pillar of our community."

"Yeah, but even with inflation figured in, he probably only leaves his waitress a quarter tip on a fifty-dollar meal."

It felt good to be laughing with Lena again.

After she left, I stretched out on the bed with a Jim Harrison novel, intending to read myself to sleep. It was no reflection on his excellent writing that I only lasted a couple of pages. All night long I dreamed of Lukas scaling the Alamo wall, dressed in dirty rags instead of his natty white suit. He was tough, all right, but I had Lena on my side.

TWELVE

You can't always tell what's going to happen.

By mid-morning the next day I found myself on another plane, headed once again for Virginia. When I'd checked in with Jim, he'd had some news—he'd come across something in Lukas's files that bore investigating. I was in Richmond in time for lunch.

We were sitting in a large booth, surrounded by jovial businessmen and businesswomen enjoying large gourmet burgers and pricey imported beers. I was so tired I knew I'd fall on my face after one swallow of alcohol, so I was sticking to coffee. Jim looked only marginally better.

"This better be good," I said, "or you just wasted four hundred and fifty dollars plus lunch. Quick flights aren't cheap."

"It's good, all right, but I'm not entirely sure what it means. It appears that my old pal hasn't been shooting straight with me."

"That's the surprise?" Where had this guy been for the last few days?

Jim wasn't to be deterred. "Remember asking me to check around to see if anything was weird in his files?"

I nodded.

"Well, yesterday I spent the better part of the afternoon in his office. Nothing seemed unusual at first. Then I found this." He handed me a document.

It was an option on a piece of property near Charlottesville. Lukas's name was on it, and someone else's I didn't recognize.

"Who's this Maupin?"

Jim shrugged. "I'm not sure. I've never heard of him, as far as I know. The one thing I am damned well sure of is that my name is nowhere on this piece of paper. Anything that important going out of this office should have my name on it."

"And you don't know anything about this property?"

He shook his head. "In fact, we have never worked out of Charlottesville before. There's been more than enough going on right here in Richmond, and we've had all the business we've needed."

He looked down at his hands. "At least, that's what I've always been led to believe." I realized then that enough had happened to Jim Cooper in the last few days to make him feel like an outsider in his own life.

This time I spoke more gently. "I don't know much about development or real estate, Jim. What does this mean, exactly?"

"One, according to our partnership agreement, we're in on everything together. Both of our names have to appear on contracts. That shows that something's not right here." He pointed to the piece of paper.

"Two, what the hell is he doing in Charlottesville? We've never done business there. It makes me wonder what else has been going on behind my back throughout the years. I feel like a damned fool."

I could certainly see his point. "You haven't heard from Lukas, have you?"

"No. It's like he just got beamed up, or something. If he knows I'm on to him, which I guess he does, he wouldn't be too likely to get in touch, I suppose. Unless he's off somewhere looking for Jesse and Greg."

Jim made a fist with his right hand and shuddered. "I'll kill him if he gets near my family again. Are you sure the boys are safe?"

106

"No problem there. They're with good friends of mine, like I said. I was careful. No one's seen them and no one's going to. Just to make sure, I've got a guard on them night and day." I smiled. "Not that the boys would ever realize they're guarded. Really, Jim, they're fine. Eugene, too."

He rubbed his eyes tiredly. "My old man. It's hard to believe I'd be putting up the dough to help save his sorry hide. Years ago, I'd've been glad to see the last of him."

"I doubt that. We think we're so tough when it comes to our feelings, but we're usually not. And Eugene's not a bad fellow these days; I've been kind of enjoying his company. Maybe old age has given him some wisdom."

Jim didn't seem too sure of that. "Maybe. Anyway, I can't think about that too much now. What's next? You gonna drive up to Charlottesville and check that out?"

"Yeah, if you could drop me off at a car-rental place. I might even get something tasteful, this time. Something befitting a gorgeous dame who's asking real-estate questions. Speaking of which, I don't know much about real estate or development, or the difference between them, for that matter. Can you give me a quick lesson? I'll just need to fake it a little." I hoped that was true.

Jim smiled. "It's not real complicated. Just think of it like this. A real-estate broker has someone who wants to sell a house. Someone else is looking for one. His job is to match them up. He gets money when that happens. Developers, on the other hand, see a piece of property they'd like to build something on. They buy it for one million, develop the property the way they intended to, and sell it for ten million. The person who sold it to them in the first place doesn't get any more money from it, period. You develop the property, you get the profit. It's as simple as that."

"So that's the reason developers are so hush-hush, then. If someone gets wind of a project before the developer's ready, it could cost him a lot more money."

"Damned straight. An overheard conversation in a restaurant or a meeting where one person runs their mouth afterwards—that's the kiss of death to a sweet deal."

"But you can be a real-estate broker and a developer at the

same time?" I was beginning to wish I'd actually taken that real-estate course my mom kept trying to push on me.

"Yeah, you can do both. But more and more, it's getting to be a conflict of interest. We do both, but the trend today is to specialize in one or the other. We actually do more brokering than development work."

"And you have no idea who Maupin is? You've never heard of him in any way?"

He shrugged. "It's a common enough name around here. Doesn't ring any bells to me."

I drained my cup of coffee and gathered up my stuff. I didn't think my brain could take in any more business details, anyway. "Okay. I've got some work to do, then. Keep your eyes open at your end, too, but keep the info to yourself. I'll stay in close touch. But meanwhile, let's go rent a car."

This time I drove away from Richmond in a silver Mercedes. I threw on some earrings while I was at it. Looking good is important in business.

Charlottesville lies about seventy miles northwest of Richmond, in the heart of central Virginia. It's a green, hilly, friendly town imbued with the presence of Thomas Jefferson, its most famous citizen.

The University of Virginia was one of the last projects completed by an aging and ailing Jefferson, and one of the three accomplishments he wanted mentioned on his tombstone. From the home he designed and built for himself on Monticello Mountain he was in command of a 360-degree view of the land, including the Blue Ridge—which really does look blue from there—gently hilly pastureland, and the town of Charlottesville. With his spyglass he could see his university and ruminate over its benefit to future generations of Virginia boys.

I took I-64 out of Richmond, a straight shot all the way. I opened the windows a bit to take in some of that sweet Virginia air and caught a bit of a WTJU radio show called *Bartender's Bop*. The disk jockey was featuring Mary Lou Williams, going back to her earliest recordings as a very young woman. He ended up with a couple of selections from her *Live in Montreux* album, recorded shortly before her death in 1981. I followed that mellow sound into town, taking an exit just past Shadwell in order to drive over Pantops Mountain.

When I was a kid Pantops was pretty bare, except for a couple of motels and a restaurant or two. People lived in the hollows around it—indeed, there was a little dirt road that incorporated a creekbed right into it. Cars drove over it slowly and carefully, most of them pausing in the middle to appreciate the view. I could remember, just barely, like an old film beginning to fade, being small and wading there, my hands reaching down through the shallow water to play with the little smooth stones while a tall adult watched over me, in case I should fall.

Much later, it was while riding down Pantops with my parents that I had first heard the Beatles playing "I Wanna Hold Your Hand," a seminal moment in my life. Now, it wouldn't even occur to you to look for a creek or a little dirt road. The whole mountain—actually a very large hill—is covered with car dealerships, shopping malls, fast-food palaces, and motels. The trick today is to ignore what's immediately in front of you coming down the hill, and to focus a little into the distance, to the greenery of the opposite hill. It's still beautiful if you know how to look. I stopped at a gas station on the 250 bypass to buy a map. Charlottesville was getting bigger every year, and I figured there would be streets that had sprung up since my time there. When I opened up the map I was sure of it. Holy shit, I thought, is this C-ville or Richmond? I turned right off the bypass onto Emmet Street, which is where Route 29 North comes into town. I drove along a good three miles without recognizing a damned thing but a sign that said "Rio Road." That's "Rio" as in "Why-O," for the uninitiated, not anything like "Rio by the Sea-O." It, too, used to be in the country, but two giant malls bordered it now, and I couldn't seem to see an end to the urban sprawl that went on and on into the horizon before me. I was looking for a certain piece of property that did not have Jim's name on it.

I finally got my bearings again when I saw a sign for the airport, where, as teenagers, we used to go out to see the few planes arrive and depart, wondering what it would be like to be on one of them. Before I knew it, I found myself within shooting distance of the piece of property specified in Lukas's agreement. I pulled off the road.

"What's the big deal?" I thought. From the car, it just looked like a big field with the ruins of a house that had mostly fallen a victim to time. Jonquils and lilac bushes still bordered the place, which was the only way I had spotted it in the first place. The red brick chimney remained, someone's workmanship defying the elements that had helped ravage the rest of the place. Tomorrow I would come out and walk the land, but for now I needed to find a room for the night. There was no time to waste.

This time I refused to stay in anything less than a hotel with a real lobby and an elevator—I'd had it with dumps that let in riffraff when you're trying to sleep. Downtown I found what I was looking for, a tasteful high-rise with a parking attendant. I thought it would do nicely for a woman looking to buy property.

I looked through my stash of business cards to find one that would do the trick. Ah, BETSY HUNT, INVESTMENTS. I'd had that one so long, I couldn't even remember where I'd gotten it. It showed a D.C. address. I pick up those cards wherever I see them, and I haven't been sorry yet.

The lobby was large, with floor-to-ceiling windows that let in a lot of sunlight. Plants hung everywhere, as did expensively framed paintings that I thought must've been chosen for their size alone. Maybe I didn't understand the complexities of modern abstract art. Watch it, Ritchie, a little voice said, Betsy Hunt probably has a condo full of this stuff. Smile knowingly, as if you were privy to a big secret. That usually works.

I paid the desk clerk in cash for the room, and tipped the bellman handsomely when he set down my bags. I was real class stuff. I looked around the room; not bad at all. From the ninth floor I could see the mountains in the distance, and all of the little people going by down below didn't look like so much as a handful of insects. I could see why power is such a seducer—it sets you apart and quite literally buys you an overview. It's no accident that rich people live at the tops of hills, poor people at the bottom.

I stripped off my clothes and laid my weary body into the sunken, rose-colored tub. The hot water made me give a little involuntary moan of pleasure. I looked around me. There were some sweet-smelling bath salts within reach and I added them to my water. Oh, but how could I have missed the bath oil right next to the shampoo on the vanity? I was sure Betsy would go ahead and use them both. I reached out a lazy arm and snaked the bath oil, too, adding it to everything else that now floated in the tub. If I was going to convince anyone I was on the prowl for expensive property, I'd better get used to grabbing the best for myself. I didn't know the real Betsy Hunt, but this one was going to be a real bitch.

When I was out of the tub and into the lush hotel robe I called room service. "This is Ms. Hunt in 901. Please bring me a bottle of Glenlivet and leave it outside my door."

They said they'd be glad to see to this at once.

"And while you're at it, how about a plate of cheese and crackers? Just start me a tab; I might be here for a few days." They assured me they could handle all of these details.

I lay back on the bed and stretched all the way to Peoria. I just hoped Betsy could hold her liquor better than she could hold her tongue, but I somehow had my doubts.

I made all the rounds, and then some. I'm not what you'd call bar crazy, but I've found many a loosened tongue among the clink of glasses. It was as good a place to start getting the pulse of the town as any. I started off in one of the hotel's bars. It was just off the left side of the lobby, dark and plush with leather chairs. Very understated. The TV over the bar was on low, with local news. A corporate type chatted me up a bit, but nothing came of it. I sipped slowly, snacking on bar nuts and getting a feel for the place. I guessed that most locals wouldn't bother with a hotel bar, unless something special was going on. I knew I was stalling, but not entirely. I was making up the rules to my game while I still had the choice.

I checked the phone book to see if some old watering spots were still around. They were. I paid my tab and went out into the night.

All in all, Betsy had one hell of an evening. At the Gaslight I gave her the opportunity to eat a filet mignon that could've been cut with a fork. That was washed down with a carafe of excellent local red wine. Virginia had gotten into wine production since I had left the state, and judging by this first taste, things were going well. After dinner I started hitting the serious bars. I knew of two that were pretty much singles bars, professionals only, no riffraff need apply. I have a long skirt I keep for just such occasions that I'd thrown into my suitcase at the last minute. I was wearing this now, along with an embroidered Mexican shirt and a turquoise necklace. I truly love turquoise and the necklace was made by a Navajo friend for me, but no one I would run into tonight would know that. What they would see instead, I hoped, was a woman bathed in money.

Starting with downtown proper, I hit one bar after another. I bought at least one drink in every place, and laughed loudly through my nose at anything that even vaguely sounded like a witticism. This kept me from looking like any kind of wallflower, and men responded as predictably as I'd expected. Lord, it really doesn't take much to play the game, I thought.

I spent a pleasant hour at Fellini's and heard some interesting stories, but none that I needed. As it grew later I abandoned downtown and headed off to the Rosewood Lounge, off 29 North. The Rosewood Lounge was notorious, a place where JAG School lawyers, conventioneers, local gentry, and local would-be's congregated, paying dearly for the opportunity. Judging by the number of cars parked out front, it looked like a good night. I chuckled when I remembered an old friend's comment about the Rosewood: "If you're rich enough you can dress down and wear jeans—everyone else has to dress up." I wondered where she'd have placed Betsy's outfit.

I sat in the Mercedes for a few minutes, taking the time to observe the natives. People tended to come out in pairs, but these weren't old couples out on the town. These people seemed to have a couple of things in common: rosy complexions from alcohol, and expensive cars. I steeled myself for drinking with the horny elite.

I opened the door to go in, and the cigarette smoke nearly

112

knocked me down. I heard laughter with a harsh edge to it and a man to my right said, smiling, "What'sa matter? Doesn't it look worth it?" I bit my tongue. He was about my age—late thirties or early forties—and I'd have bet money he was a UVA alumnus. UVA was called the Princeton of the South, and as such affected its own version of Ivy League dress, which hadn't changed much with the times, right down to the Bass Weejuns on the man's feet. I sighed inwardly as I forced up a smile of my own. "I should probably just buy a pack myself. Might as well give in."

That was unfortunate wording, because the man smirked or smiled, no telling which. "Giving in already? What exciting news. And to think that I was just about to go home a few minutes ago."

I groaned. "Where did you learn to talk to women—a charm school for Huns?" I hadn't meant to say it, but the man laughed and I thought, "Okay—maybe I've found Betsy's style."

He gave me a mock bow. "Please don't let my bad manners run you off. I'm usually every bit a gentleman. Let me buy you a drink and you'll see."

He was as good as any, I thought. We grabbed a couple of seats near the piano, which was being played competently, if not with feeling, by someone who looked young enough to be putting himself through school this way. Midway through my Glenlivet I regretted my choice of drinking companions. He was an engineer who had originally come to Charlottesville to attend UVA and had stayed. His wife was a bitch who didn't have her priorities straight, his kid was spoiled, and I would have bet his own dog couldn't stand the sight of him. I was beginning to see why. Even with liquor in my system he was boring the bejesus out of me. His voice droned on in the background while I looked around me. All I had to do was mutter an "okay" or "hmmm" every now and then and he took it as real encouragement. Suddenly I realized he had stopped talking and was looking at me expectantly.

"Sorry," I muttered. "I was just looking for a clock."

"It's around midnight. I asked you what you did for a living."

"I'm in investments. Usually I work out of the D.C. area, but every now and then I simply must visit the provinces, you know. See what the common people are doing." I laughed airily, or Betsy did. Fortunately the guy didn't ask me what "investments" entailed. I'd barely passed high school math.

When someone he knew came in I extracted myself by heading for the ladies' room. I sat there in an overstuffed chair for a few minutes, hoping his attention span was as short as I'd judged it to be. When I rounded the bar I saw he'd trapped another fly, who appeared to be just drunk enough to tolerate his company. She laughed at something he said, and his arm went around her. I glanced at the clock and made a silent bet: ten minutes and they'd be gone.

After a while I wondered why I didn't go to bars more often; they were wonderful places in which to observe the human condition in some of its more laughable guises. One fellow walked up to every woman sitting or standing alone, and said something low to her. When he got to me, I found out what it was: "I'm Royce Harrington. Would you like to go home with me?"

I laughed. "Does that ever work?"

"Has until now," he said, and moved on down the bar. Three women away, he struck gold. A fortyish blonde looked him over and nodded. They were gone in five minutes.

I eavesdropped shamelessly. Some friends crowded around the curved end of the bar accidentally fed me choice bits of local gossip. They talked animatedly about a scandal involving a university professor who had recently been caught with a local teenager, and let's just say all of their clothes were not on. I was shocked.

At about one o'clock I couldn't take any more and headed back to the hotel for some sleep. The bars were a good place for information, all right, but tomorrow I'd have to work on a faster way to extract it.

I woke up the next morning at ten and sat down at the desk to plan out my day. I knew a pub near Court Square that served huge sandwiches to the lawyers, real-estate guys, and newspaper reporters who worked nearby. In the old days—I wasn't sure about now—it had also been the place to go for the several-martini lunch. Since liquor and tongue-wagging are practically inseparable, the place was definitely on my agenda. I also planned to go out to the property off 29 North later.

The Fox's Den was humming when I walked in at twelve-thirty. The place is in the heart of the historic district; the red bricks were soft-looking with age, not so much red as brownish finally. The place had been here since a little after Jefferson's day. Some of its patrons had been here for nearly that long, too, judging by the proprietary way they took their seats, waiting wordlessly for their unordered drinks to arrive.

I sat at a high stool at the bar and ordered a corned beef on rye and a Coke. The sandwiches were still enormous and excellent, and the crowd was much as I remembered it, with the addition of more women. It had been a men's place when I used to know it, intimidating as hell to a shy young woman.

The bartender, who seemed to know most people in the room, had been giving me interested glances for a bit so I decided to start right there. I ordered a coffee. "What's going on in town, these days? I used to live here but now it's like another country."

He smiled nicely, his bushy black mustache giving him the look of a happy walrus, if a walrus ever had a neat-looking ponytail and an earring. "Depends on what you're into, I suppose. Different people would tell you different things." He set my cup of coffee down before me and leaned on the cherrywood bar.

Close to the vest was okay—I could even admire it. "Who's doing the malls and shopping centers out off Twenty-nine? I could hardly recognize the place."

"Oh, mostly a handful of investors from D.C. who like the idea of the quiet country lifestyle C-ville's known for. Thought it could stand a little jazzing up, I guess."

I nodded. "Well, they must've turned a pretty profit for their work. There were lots of cars in every parking lot I saw, and that always means money changing hands."

He shrugged and looked over his shoulder to see if anyone needed his services. He turned back to me. "I haven't seen you here before. Did you just move back to town?"

"I haven't actually moved here yet, though I am considering it," I lied. I've never found it all that hard; it's kind of like acting, which I enjoy. "Actually, I'm here on business." I stuck out my hand. "My name is Betsy Hunt."

He shook my hand warmly. "My name's Nick Papolonis."

"Nick the Greek, huh? How'd you wind up here in WASP-Land?"

He laughed. "My cousins own a restaurant here. I used to come down here summers when I was a kid in Jersey. One day I found myself without any immediate plans and said, 'What the hey?' Charlottesville had always been kind of a refuge for me, and I thought, Why not?"

"And has it been good for you?"

He nodded. "It's really been okay. I'm not making a pile of money, but then I'm not a very mercenary guy."

That was refreshing, these days. I almost felt bad about lying to the man.

"So, Betsy, what're you doing here?"

I smiled cagily. "I'm in investments up in D.C." It was certainly starting to trip lightly enough off the tongue. "I just thought I'd come down for a few days and look around for a business opportunity or two. You know, kind of branch out."

He looked thoughtful. "Investments, huh? Is that how you people usually operate? Sounds more casual than I would've thought."

"Well, Nick, I guess I'd have to admit it's not the way everyone in the business works, but that's certainly been my style up till now. I can't say I've ever regretted it yet."

"So who do you know here? Anyone I'd have heard of?"

I shrugged. "Probably not. But look"—I smiled big—"I know you now, don't I? That's progress. After all, I just got here."

"For what it's worth, I'd be happy to be of service. Plenty of hotshots come here all the time." He looked around. An elderly man with a headful of white hair looked up from a lively conversation and winked at Nick, then smiled. Nick made a pistol with forefinger and thumb and mock-shot it at the dignified-looking man, who laughed and said something to his companion, who also laughed. It looked like an old joke to me.

Nick turned back to me. "That's Morton Davis. He's head of Davis Enterprises, and one of the wealthiest men around here. He's

116

actually quite a nice fellow, if you can live with a racial joke every now and then."

I couldn't, but Betsy probably could, if it meant money. "Could you introduce me to him, Nick?" There's waiting around, and then there's plunging in.

Nick looked at me with a penetrating gaze. "Will you swear to me you're on the up and up? This better not be some scam. I'm not a rube from the country, you know; I'm from Jersey. I've got a reputation to maintain."

"Nick, believe me, you won't have to worry about a man of Davis's importance. He'd smell a scam a mile off. I just want to play nice, and meet some folks I could do business with." I smiled. "C'mon, what harm's an introduction? He'll check me out before he finishes shaking my hand."

Nick laughed. "Okay, wait here for a sec."

He was gone for an eternity, although the clock said just a couple of minutes had passed. I kept custody of the eyes, but could see, with peripheral vision, a brief exchange taking place between the two seated men and Nick. Then Nick came back and said, "Mr. Davis asks if you'd like to join him for a drink at his table."

I let my breath out slowly.

After introductions and drink orders Davis and his friend discreetly looked me over. "Ms. Hunt, how could we be of assistance to you? Nick says you're into investments, is that right?"

I held my nose and jumped into the water. "That's right. Up in D.C. Some of my clients wish to branch out, and I know that Charlottesville is a growing, expanding town. I was hoping to find something for them here." I paused. "Say, a piece of property off Twenty-nine North, maybe. Or up around the airport, if there's anything going on of interest."

Davis looked at his friend, a nondescript man named Perkins or Parkins, I hadn't caught which. "You want to develop some property, is that right?"

"Well, not personally, you understand. Some clients have heard about some land out near the airport that is being sold, as I understand. I thought if it was anything of real interest someone would've heard about it."

Davis thought a minute. "Can you tell me more specifically where the land is? I know that area fairly well."

I told him.

He looked at me in puzzlement. "Sounds like the Maupin property to me. I doubt it would be for sale—we've all tried to buy it, certainly, but it's family land and the man just doesn't want to sell. I have to respect that. Too many people can be bought nowadays."

He seemed sincere. This made me wonder even more what Lukas had cooked up.

"Well, thanks for the info. I guess my informants were wrong. Oh, well—that happens, sometimes." I took a sip of my drink.

Davis eyed me neutrally. "Ms. Hunt, perhaps you know an old friend of mine in Washington. He's in investments also—Garnett Dupré."

I swallowed. Should I bite or not? I took a chance. "Why, yes, I do, as a matter of fact. Garnett and I have had dealings more than once; how nice that you know him also."

Davis stood up abruptly and an ugly red crept up his neck. If looks could kill, I didn't have long to live.

"Ms. Hunt, or whoever you are, you can get the hell away from my table before I have you checked out by the police. Garnett Dupré is a friend of mine, all right, but he's a restaurateur in New Orleans. And if I were you, I'd learn the correct way to do business if you're going to impersonate an investment banker."

Well, what could I do? I fled. Nick looked at me curiously as I skulked out the door, but I wasn't exactly dawdling. I wasn't sure about Betsy Hunt anymore, but Lil Ritchie was starting to have fun. There's planning the stew, and then there's throwing everything you've got into the pot to see what you can come up with. Like gumbo.

"Score one for Ritchie," I said silently. I had a feeling things were just starting to cook.

This time, instead of visiting the property I decided to visit the neighbors. I drove slowly; it was a pretty day, sunny and in the lower seventies. I'd thrown a handful of tapes into my suitcase the day before, and now I stuck one of them into the tape deck: Ray Charles, with one of his combos from the early sixties, playing a mix of jazz and low-down blues. Brother Ray, both cool and hot, accompanied me all the way out to the turnoff to the airport.

This time I paid more attention to the lay of the land. A few houses hugged in close to the road, with an occasional farmhouse set back into some trees. The trees tended to be large old oaks—real grandfather trees—with black walnuts, mimosas, sycamores and magnolias adding color and flavor. I didn't know how I'd managed to get a real hit of an early Virginia spring; I just thanked my lucky stars.

I stopped at a house directly across the road from Lukas's property, but no one answered, no dogs barked, and there were no cars in the driveway. Oh well, I thought, I could always try again.

I had better luck when I pulled into the yard of the farmhouse just down the road, still in sight of the land in question. Two pickups and a Dodge sedan were in the driveway, and this time two dogs—a collie mix and a beagle—came out to greet me, sniffing eagerly and wagging their tails furiously. I didn't think I had anything to fear. I squatted down to pat them and heard footsteps on the porch. I stood up. A woman, sixtyish, had come out to see what I wanted.

I gave her my trust-me smile. "Sorry to bother you, but I'm trying to locate the person who owns the piece of property down the road." I pointed.

She frowned slightly. "I hope there's nothing wrong. There's not, is there?"

Now why would she think that? I shook my head. "Not that I know of. I'm representing some people interested in possibly purchasing the land, that's all. Would you know who I should get in touch with?"

She nodded briefly. "That would be Mr. Maupin, but I've heard he's been sick, you know. Up till now, he's done pretty well for someone his age, but I heard he's gone back something awful since his wife, Rebecca, died in January." She shrugged philosophically. "That's life, I guess. All of us have to go down that road if we live long enough."

119

Or why do we call it the blues, I thought. I could feel a vague depression descending upon me, floating down from that clean white porch.

"Did you know the property was for sale?"

"Well, is it? Are you sure it actually is?"

"Yes, ma'am, I believe it is. Could you tell me how to get in touch with this Mr. Maupin?"

She frowned again. "Let me see—I have his number here somewhere in the house. I think you could write him in care of his son, John Junior, if Mr. Maupin Senior is too sick to handle his affairs." She leaned toward me conspiratorially and lowered her voice. "He's a very successful man, that John Junior, as I understand it."

Now, that was interesting. "Does Mr. Maupin live with his son, then?"

"No, it's the other way around. There's an old family house—kind of a mansion, I guess you'd call it—that Mr. Maupin and his wife kept up for as long as they could. It's out there near Free Union. When she got too sick to run the household, John Junior and his wife moved in and kind of took over the running of it. That's what I understand, anyway. I'm a little out of date, probably, but I think if things were much different, I would've heard something. Mr. Maupin's fondly known to a lot of people."

"Was this property here an old family home? Looks like it's been abandoned for some time."

"Oh, that place goes way back. It's been in Mr. Maupin's family for generations, probably since colonial times almost. I understand the place was in the middle of some battle in the War Between the States." She laughed. "Not that my family was here then. We stuck it out in Ireland as long as we had potatoes. When they ran out, I guess traveling started looking a little better."

"That would do it, all right," I said. "Mrs.—" I hesitated.

"Reed," she said. "Ellen Reed, or Mrs. Thurston Reed, whichever one anybody calls me, I'll answer to. I'm as proud of my husband's name as any, not like these young girls today, all angry and full of themselves."

Let's not get into this now, I thought. No differences of

opinion allowed when pumping a witness while impersonating someone else altogether. It's one of my rules. I wondered if Mrs. Reed had noticed I wasn't wearing a bra.

"Mrs. Reed, if you wouldn't mind getting me any address you might have, I'd certainly appreciate it. I promise not to be bothering you again."

She went into the house for almost ten minutes, but not before leaving me with some iced tea and an invitation to have a seat on the front steps. I drank the delicious tea—nice and sugary like my mom's—and patted the dogs some more. They licked me gratefully and left huge trails of dog drool up and down my forearms and legs. If this kept up much longer I'd have to go inside for a shower.

Mrs. Reed came out and handed me a piece of paper with a phone number and address on it. I thanked her. "I hope this helps," she said. "The old place used to be a family farm, I understand, way back then. It would be nice to see it farmed again, but I don't suppose your people plan on doing anything that simple with it. It wouldn't much fit the times." She sighed.

I smiled at her, and meant it this time. "These times aren't everything they're cracked up to be, are they? I miss seeing farms, myself."

I looked around at her well-kept house and barn, into the hayfield that adjoined the Maupins' property. A handful of Guernseys could be seen in the pasture beyond the house, munching and chewing, morning snacktime lasting through lunch. I really did miss seeing more farms. It seemed lately that most of the ones I did see had FOR SALE signs tacked to a post. I looked up at the woman. "I'd certainly hope that anyone who bought this land would respect what it's been up until now."

She shrugged again, someone who'd learned to become a fatalist when it came to the intentions of others in the late twentieth century. "I just can't believe Mr. Maupin would ever turn over that place, that's all. He's told me any number of times this would always be in his family. It made him real happy to know that. As sick as he is, I can't believe he'd ever turn it loose. He's always been a man who could make up his mind and stick to it."

I wondered if the son had inherited his old man's strong desire for continuity. Maybe that would be worth some checking into. One thing was for sure—*some* Maupin had made a deal with Donny Lukas. I intended to find out who. After that, I'd work on why.

Brother Ray and I headed back down the road.

THIRTEEN

I went back to my hotel room and called Molly at work. She answered right away and I said, "This is Ms. Betsy Hunt and I'd like to speak with the best quack you've got."

She didn't miss a beat. "The best quack I know is out of town right now, God knows where."

"God knows best," I said. "Maybe you could help me, then."

"Lil, I'm glad you called; I was getting worried about you. Where are you now?"

"I'm such a globe-trotter, it's kind of hard to say. Any news up there?"

"You'd better believe it. You remember I told you I'd have someone check on the trailer regularly, right? Well, two nights ago someone broke in and searched the place—ransacked it, really. I don't know if anything was taken, but it's not because someone didn't try."

Shit. Was Lukas that close behind? "Are you sure it wasn't just some kids looking for a stereo?"

"Well, a neighbor, a Mr. Seth Jordan, was walking his dog around nine o'clock that night, before he went to bed, and saw a car parked along the road right where Eugene's path starts. He noticed it especially, for a couple of reasons: One, Eugene doesn't get many visitors; two, it had Virginia tags. As you know, winter is not when we get our Southern visitors here in the North Country."

I felt a chill go up my backbone. "Did you report it to the cops? Did Mr. Jordan?"

"Mr. Jordan didn't know anything more than the part about the car. My friend Rudy was checking on the place for me and found the break-in later. Since he *is* a cop, well, he didn't exactly have to report it."

Rudy was a buddy of hers. They played poker once a week— they had for years—and I wasn't sure what else. I knew this much: He'd been of unofficial help more than once.

"Did Rudy dust for prints or anything?"

"Yeah, but he didn't find anything. As you know, I couldn't, as an officer of the court, interfere with the criminal-justice system. Rudy just told the sheriff he'd been keeping an eye on the place because he knew Eugene was gone. It wasn't really a lie. He just didn't mention my name, and knew better than to ask me if you were involved. If anybody suspects it, they haven't said so to me. Anyway, we closed the place back up and put a board up where they'd broken a window to get in."

Poor Eugene. He didn't have much to start with; now maybe what he did have was ruined. "Was everything really trashed?"

"Pretty much. You know, I think these guys get a kick out of doing that stuff. Probably were toilet-trained badly."

"You said 'guys,' plural. Do you know that for a fact?"

"Yeah. Rudy showed me the two sets of boot prints."

Okay, I thought. "Molly, I called to check on what was happening up there, and to also ask you a couple of questions about real estate and title stuff."

"Shoot. What I don't know, I can find out."

"Well, first, can it be fixed up somehow for a piece of property to stay in a family forever, more or less?"

"Well, no, not exactly. It would be up to each generation to keep up their end of the bargain. For instance, a father could will

124

his property to his son or daughter, who hopefully would leave it to his or her children in turn. Sort of like that. But anything more would be ruling from the grave."

"Heaven forbid. So if the son or whoever had other ideas, even though he knew his father's wishes, he could go against the will and do anything he wanted with the property? Nothing could be done in a court of law?"

"There's certainly nothing illegal about it if he has title or can act for the owner, but morally or ethically he would need to examine his conscience."

That was all I needed to know. "Is there someplace I could look up the information about the title? And would an option to buy be a matter of public record?"

"Well, strictly speaking, any change should be recorded with the Registry of Deeds. Sometimes it may not show up right away, though; these things happen. The transaction's not legally binding unless the change is recorded, though. Anyone can go look that up, but just make sure it's someone who understands legal gobbledygook and the state law."

Did she think I couldn't? "Molly, did I ever tell you how smart and helpful you are?" I hit my stride. "And what a truly great best friend you are?"

"Cut the crap, Ritchie. You always have used my superior knowledge for your own greedy purposes, and we both know it. It's just that I feel sorry for you."

"Good," I said. "Pity is good, too. Whatever it takes to have your full cooperation in my life. Speaking of which, how's my most beautiful friend?"

She laughed, the best sound I'd heard for some time. "Littlefield? He's fine. I took him some of the catnip from Robin's land—you know, that stuff's more powerful than anything they sell in the stores. He went wild and went on a claw-to-claw furniture kill that would've appalled a lesser man than Fred. Fred just thought it was funny and said he was gonna cook up some chicken livers for Littlefield while he was still in the clutches of his narcotic high." She laughed again. "What a man, that Fred. His mama certainly must've raised him right."

125

"Actually, I met her once. She's an interesting woman."

"Lil, are you ever coming back? We miss you."

I couldn't think of that now. "I'll be back pretty soon, I think, but I don't know when. Things seem to be moving along pretty fast, though."

"Just be careful. Remember you're only one part super-woman—the other part's a major klutz."

Huh, I thought, as I hung up my end of the phone. I have the natural grace of a Gene Kelly. That woman must be blind.

I didn't waste any time. I called up my old high school friend Gordon—the guy who recommended me to Jim Cooper—who said he'd arrange for a young attorney he knew to check the deed at the registry. The gobbledygook taken care of, I drove off to have a talk with a sick old man.

It was still a beautiful day, and as I drove toward Free Union, I remembered why it was one of my favorite areas of Virginia. Lovely estates bordered the somewhat narrow road, with impeccably white fences giving the land a sense of order. Already green at this time of year, the fields went almost as far as the eye could see, sloping gently here and there. Handsome horses were in some of the pastures, expensive-looking cattle in the others. A lot of Albemarle County is known for horse and cattle breeding, and steeplechase racing is a popular event throughout the spring and summer, as is the fox hunt in the fall. The closest most ordinary people get to all this, of course, is a glance out the window on the way to and from work, but I was glad it was all there, just the same. Beauty is beauty, I thought.

The drive out didn't take me long. I stopped off at a general store for a Coke—one of those little bottles I only seem to find in the South—and directions to the old man's house. Virginians don't say everything they mean, not by a long shot, but I thought I detected a note of concern for Mr. Maupin Senior. Junior got a different response. When I asked how he was faring these days, the storekeeper stiffened slightly and said something pleasant enough, but his eyes froze me out from that moment on. I said polite good-byes and took the hint.

The estate was called Willow Green, and it was easy to see why. The house was an old white brick from the late 1700s, if I was guessing right. You could see it from the main road, but just barely. A small creek cut across the property from just behind the house, and meandered down the sloping hill toward the road I was on. Willows, large and lovely as they are only in the South, had been planted alongside the creek a long time ago, and they'd been well cared for. A blooming tulip poplar caught my eye as I started slowly up the driveway. The house itself was surrounded by huge old oaks, planted in the days before fans and air conditioning, when they would have been the only source of cool air and a breeze at night. I would've bet that it was a good ten degrees cooler under those trees on a hot day.

The driveway was a circular deal, up by the house. There was only one car parked there, a far-from-new Plymouth. I parked behind it and the thought struck me that I didn't really have a plan for how to talk to Mr. Maupin. Certainly this was sticky business and I didn't want to upset a man who was already down. It's at times like this that you have to rely on experience, though. I took a deep breath and knocked on the door.

It was opened by a woman who was obviously in the middle of something. She frowned almost imperceptibly when she saw me, then remembered her manners almost as fast and smiled, a brief flicker in a concerned face. Her high cheekbones and her skin the color of rich milk chocolate made her a natural beauty, as did her kind-looking eyes. She had the look of someone more used to smiling than not.

"Hello," she said now. "How may I help you?"

I tried out a smile myself. "My name is Betsy Hunt, and I'd like to see Mr. Maupin Senior, if I may. It's a small business matter." I showed her Betsy's card.

"Ms. Hunt, I don't mean to seem officious, but I'm not sure that this is a very good time for Mr. Maupin. He's not at all well."

I nodded. "I realize that, but I promise I won't take up much of his time. It's a matter of some importance, or I wouldn't bother him at all." I tried appealing to her goodwill. "I really am sorry for coming here unannounced. It's just that I'm interested in a piece of property he owns, and I need to speak to him directly about it."

That seemed to be the wrong thing to say.

"Ms."—she paused to glance again at my card—"Hunt, Mr. Maupin is a very sick elderly gentleman who is not even in the real-estate business. Suddenly the whole world acts as if he were fully capable of putting in a working day, which I assure you he is not. To put it honestly, he's as upset as he can be, right at this minute. I, in all conscience, cannot show an utter stranger back to his room under these circumstances. I'm sorry, but I don't think it would be a good idea." She looked as though her mind was made up.

I decided then and there to take the direct approach.

"Suppose my business with him is just what he needs? Suppose Mr. Maupin has fallen on hard times, through no fault of his own. Sometimes relatives, the most well-meaning ones, even, aren't always the best of help in a crisis."

I met her startled look and knew I'd scored a point. I kept on going. "What if I'm the person who can make Mr. Maupin's life mean something again? I promise you, I'm not trouble. I'm probably the only chance he's got." I let my words sink in.

I'd obviously struck some kind of nerve. Suddenly, this confident woman seemed uncertain of her next move. She looked at me quietly, sizing me up.

"You're no 'finance' person, are you?" she said quietly.

I had to make another quick decision. "No," I admitted. "I'm a private detective. I'm working on a case that, more and more, appears to involve Mr. Maupin's interests."

"What is your real name, then?"

I took out my I.D. "Ritchie. Lil Ritchie." I offered my hand. She hesitated for a mere heartbeat before accepting. Her grip was warm and firm.

"My name is Dora. Mrs. Dora Jones. I've been Mr. Maupin's housekeeper for years, and by now we mean an awful lot to each other. I'm kind of all he's got left."

She opened the door wider and stepped aside. "Have a seat in the parlor there." She made a sweeping motion with her arm toward the room just to the right of the hallway. "I'll tell Mr. Maupin you're here."

I started to obey, thankful that I'd gotten this far. Then I noticed she hadn't yet moved from her spot at the entrance of the room. "Mrs. Jones, is there something else you need to tell me?" Call it instinct.

She nodded. "He got a phone call a couple of days ago that has simply put him into a tailspin. He won't talk, not even to me. Something's terribly wrong. Just last week he was sick, to be sure, but peaceful in his heart. Now he's like a man possessed. He hates the very sight of his son and his daughter-in-law, all of a sudden." She looked at me, her face full of concern. "The man's in anguish, that's all I know, and I'm very afraid for him."

I could see that. "Thanks," I said. "That's useful information. How was Mr. Maupin's relationship with the son and his wife before this recent upset?"

She sighed. "It was okay. Mr. Maupin is a fine old man, and he was a fine younger man. His wife was a good Christian woman also, kindness personified. I've known John Junior since he was a boy, and he's never been the son they expected to have. He was a difficult child, and he's a difficult man. Mr. Maupin loves him because he's his flesh and blood, but I do know he's had to live with his disappointment for many years. He's made do, is all."

I wondered how far John Junior would go to be his own man. "I assume no one's in the house other than us, is that right?" I didn't want to meet this son before I was ready.

Dora nodded. "Yes, that much I know, at least. Neither John Junior nor Sharon gets home until late, often having had dinner in town. There'll be no one here for a good two or three hours, at the earliest."

I thought of something. "Do you think you could get me a photo of John Junior? It could come in handy."

"I suppose I could find a snapshot around here someplace, if you really think it's necessary."

I nodded once, readying myself. "Okay, let's get this done, then."

She paused for another moment. "Miss Ritchie, I hope I

haven't done the wrong thing. I did right to trust you, didn't I?"

"I certainly believe you did. I'll give it all I've got; that much I can promise."

She turned around and this time left the room. I could hear her footsteps receding as she walked down the hall. Then I was alone.

The room I was eventually shown into was toward the back of the house, a large old-fashioned master bedroom with heavy dark furniture, mahogany and walnut being the woods I could identify. Mr. Maupin himself lay upon a four-poster bed that seemed to swallow him up; he was that frail. I hoped he would be up for what I needed to have him say.

The man I saw had been strikingly handsome. His hair was longish, and snow-white. He had a full mustache, also white, that made him look dashing. His blue eyes gave him away, though. They were filled with pain that I knew to come from more than one source. It's probably cancer, I thought, now this.

He gestured toward me with impatience. "Come over here where I can see you," he said.

I walked over to the bed and his eyes appraised me as I stood there, uncertain of my next move. Finally he pointed to an over-stuffed chair by his bedside. "Sit," he said. "Dora says you can help me."

Thank God for Dora, I thought. This man was an imposing presence, sick or not. "Well, let me put it this way, Mr. Maupin. I think we each have things to say that the other needs to hear."

He sighed, a long and painful shudder. "Young lady, I have cancer of the lungs. I smoked three packs of cigarettes a day, and when I stopped that I switched over to cigars. Now breathing at all is getting to be entirely too much trouble. Spit it out. I haven't got a lot of time, as you can see."

He had a point. "Okay, then. I'm protecting some people from a fellow named Lukas. He's killed before, and his fingers are in a lot of different pies down in Richmond. Just recently his partner found an option he'd signed on a piece of property in this area. It was on your family land out near the airport. Did you sign that paper, Mr. Maupin?"

He closed his eyes, and for a few distressing moments I thought he'd fallen asleep. He hadn't though. When he opened them up again I realized he'd been summoning the physical strength to get through the next few minutes.

"No," he said, "I most certainly did not. My son, John Junior, has power of attorney and he did this on his own."

"Against your wishes." I wanted to hear it out loud.

"It was over my dead body, more or less. I found out just a few days ago. An old friend I've known for fifty years still works at the registry office downtown. He called me in disbelief when the option was registered. My son doesn't know this. He's not"— he hesitated—"very observant."

"Are you going to stop him? This land is important to you, I gather."

He looked at me mournfully. "It's important to us all, young lady. It represents history."

"Because it's old?"

He shook his head violently. "No! Because it's hallowed ground! It's our heritage, and it's being squandered for God knows what piece of trash."

What effort this cost the old man, I could only guess. "What is this land, then, Mr. Maupin?"

He looked at me, eyes fierce as a hawk's.

"Do you have an interest in history, young lady? Or does it mean anything to young people these days? Do you care that people have died to give us our liberty?" He shook his head in disgust. "Probably not," he said softly. "Probably not."

I leaned in toward him. "I care, or I wouldn't be bothering you right now. I'd like to hear about this land of yours."

He allowed himself a minute to sort out what he wanted to say. I sat back in the chair, meanwhile, determined to stay for as long as it took. Finally he was ready. With his eyes closed, he began to talk.

★　★　★

"In 1864, this countryside was devastated by the war. Virginia had taken a beating for three years so far, and it wasn't over until everything we had was gone. My family lived on that piece of land, as they had since the late 1700s. My ancestor Thaddeus Maupin created a farm long ago out of forest—*forest*—you can't possibly know how hard that was. None of us work that hard nowadays."

I nodded in encouragement.

"On June eleventh and twelfth, 1864, Union cavalry under the command of General Phil Sheridan fought a battle west of here in Louisa County, at a place called Trevilian Station. He had two things on his mind: to cripple the railroad at Gordonsville, a major railroad center during the war; and to connect with General David Hunter in Charlottesville. They didn't know what they were getting into, because they had two days of bloody fighting on their hands in what turned out to be the fiercest all-cavalry battle of the war. It cost everyone involved plenty—two thousand men in all. They never were able to get to Gordonsville, and Hunter wasn't in Charlottesville as Sheridan had thought, but rather in Lynchburg, being a major pain in the behind."

"What did this have to do with your family land?"

"I'm getting to that. Could you tell me your name again?"

I told him. "Well, Miss Ritchie, a little-known historical fact is that a band of Union cavalry soldiers under a Major Jubal Harris headed toward Charlottesville on their way to Waynesboro, to join what was happening in the Shenandoah Valley. The Shenandoah Valley was known as the breadbasket of the Confederacy, and you'd better believe the basket was almost empty at that point. General David Hunter and his eighteen thousand troops had been up and down the valley, destroying every bit of property they could get their hands on. Our people were counting on those supplies. Things were rough.

"Well, this Major Harris and his troops rode up into my great-grandfather's farm, which was made up at that point of women, children, and old folks like me now. They scared my great-grandmother nearly to death, and demanded to be fed and housed until they could go farther." He glanced over at me. "In their defense, Miss Ritchie, it was wartime and they were exhausted, sick, and hungry, just as my grandfather and his men were, in the valley.

"The Union men stayed for three days. They didn't hurt anyone, but the threat was there. They were desperate. On June seventeenth or so, a band of Confederate soldiers happened to be returning home for a much-needed few days of rest. They were going to try to scrounge some supplies to take back to the other men they'd left in the valley. What can I say but that, as fate would have it, they spotted a friendly farmhouse and went there in search of food and shelter. They were not expecting to see the enemy, and the enemy was certainly not expecting them."

I found myself sitting on the edge of my seat.

"Well, a battle ensued that left a good many on both sides dead, my grandmother among them. She was hit in the head by a bullet that, I imagine, missed its mark. The homeplace was burned down to the ground. When Thaddeus Maupin came home, it was as a widower. He'd lost the war, his wife, and his home. Try to imagine that," Maupin said.

"And this is the land your son has agreed to sell to Donald Lukas."

"Yes. I had known this family history always. My mother told me the story over and over again when I was a child, and my father talked about it as if it had just happened yesterday. It meant something. It never got more than a mention in the history books; there were so many other battles that were bigger.

"A few months ago a man came to see me out of the blue, just like you. He showed up at the door on a winter's day. It turned out he was a descendant of Major Jubal Harris. He's much younger than I, but like me, had grown up with this story too, in Pennsylvania. He came here to convince me to help make that piece of land an official part of our history. He wanted me to deed the land over to a trust in order to do what was necessary to make it an official Civil War battlefield site. I agreed. His ancestor had fought and died there, too. I'd never been so glad to hear a suggestion in my life. John Junior didn't need the land. I'm leaving him well off. It seemed to be the thing to do."

I nodded. It made sense to me, too. "And did you tell your son about this change?"

"Why yes, I did. He took it hard, quite unexpectedly. He'd never had any interest in the property or the family stories. I thought as long as I intended to leave him with a good inheritance it was my business." Maupin laughed, a hollow sound full of pain and bitterness. "I was wrong. He wanted it all, I guess, and he's figured a way to get it."

"But you just found out about the option? You never signed a document giving your son the land?"

"I signed an agreement giving him power of attorney, which has turned out to be the same thing, hasn't it? I'm too sick and tired to fight it."

"What if someone fought it for you, Mr. Maupin? I'm sure something could still be done. Lukas is on the run, so nothing can happen right away, as it is. That buys you a little time."

"Time," he mused. "That's not something I can afford to play around with, you know. Used to be there was all the time in the world, but no more."

I said nothing. He was right.

I was curious about one thing. "Mr. Maupin, why didn't your family rebuild on that land? Why has it stayed just the way it was left? Surely your family would've wanted to stay on the ancestral land."

He gave a little shrug. "My grandfather turned into a bitter man. He didn't want that reminder to go away. He wanted us to know what we had lost." He looked out his window for a few seconds. "I'm not sure he was right."

Mr. Maupin lay there quietly for a bit, and I could tell he had fallen into an old man's memories. "John's never been happy, never been satisfied. He's had every advantage but he's never done anything with them. He married a nice girl from a poor but well-thought-of family in Greene County. She thought he was the greatest catch she could possibly get. She was wrong. He got her young and gave her the same goals he's set for himself, whatever those are. He just wants and wants. Sharon goes along with it, but she's not been her own person since she came to us as a young, impressionable girl. I wouldn't be surprised if she's afraid of him. I look at her and don't see a center."

"Mr. Maupin, if I can find a way to put a stop to what's happened, could you live with your son's disappointment?"

"Miss Ritchie, I'm an old man who's not going to live very much longer, no matter what's going on in this world. But this is wrong—he's robbing this nation's future children of part of their heritage." He leveled a piercing gaze at me. "You and I know there'll be precious little left for the generations to come, as it is. We've fouled our own nest, so to speak."

I couldn't disagree.

"Do you know what this man Lukas wants with the land?"

I shook my head. "It'll all come out, eventually. If things go the way I think they will, Lukas won't touch your land, Mr. Maupin. I think it's a little too late for him to follow through with his plan."

He sighed and closed his eyes again. "I hope you'll forgive me, but I'm suddenly very, very tired. Could we continue this on another day? You could come out after my son leaves, some morning."

"I wouldn't miss it for the world," I said. I put my hand on his bony old arm. "You get some rest, now. You know the tides of history can get turned by such small acts as yours. Don't give up hope."

I handed him my phone number at the hotel. "Call me if you need anything."

He opened his eyes again and a small smile played at the corners of his mouth. "I see you still have the idealism of youth." He patted my hand. "We'll see, Miss Ritchie, we'll see."

When I left he looked like no more than a ripple in the blankets.

We would see, indeed.

FOURTEEN

I rapped on the window at the Fox's Den; Nick looked up. He saw who it was and went on with his polishing. His back gave me the message: "You blew it, lady."

This time I went to the door and tried the knob. Someone had forgotten to lock up before closing; being an opportunist, I walked right in.

"I don't wanna talk to you. You made me look like an asshole in front of my best customers. What do you think, I'm suicidal?"

"No," I said, "just trusting. Which is why I'm here now. I shouldn't have done that to you, Nick. I'm sorry."

He looked at me coolly for a bit before resuming the cleaning of his bar glasses. "You're damned right you shouldn't. I don't know why I'm even talking to you right now. You're apparently not who you said you were, anyway."

"Well, if you'll let me buy you dinner, I promise I'll come clean. How about it, Nick? Let me make it up to you. Then, if you don't want anything else to do with me I won't bother you again. Scout's honor."

"Hmph," he said. "I don't know who the hell you are, but

you've never been a Scout. I was one, so I should know. I'm a team player, while you're some kind of hot-dog adrenaline freak, and that's if I'm lucky. Am I right?"

He looked so mad I had to laugh. "C'mon, Nick. Meet me at Random Row in an hour. Holding on to anger's no good. Let me buy you some beers instead."

"You're paying? Tips weren't what they usually are today, for some reason." He narrowed his eyes at me, but I could see he wasn't really mad at me anymore.

I waited.

"Okay, I'll go, but don't try anything slick. That's where my friends hang out."

"That's okay by me. Friends are just what I need."

An hour later found me showered and changed into jeans and a light flannel shirt. I was tired of Betsy Hunt and her pretensions.

As I walked into the restaurant I felt a lightness of heart I hadn't had the luxury of feeling in a good while. This was one of my favorite hangouts in the old days, and I could tell at once it hadn't turned into something else in the years I'd been gone. Good food smells were in the air, and the people at the bar were enjoying an after-work beer or two. Nick was sitting alone at a table not too close to the bar. It looked like a good place to talk.

The waitress came over. She had a Virginia accent you couldn't cut with a machete. "We're gonna eat, but let me have a Beck's first, please." I smiled at her. "We might need a few minutes." She took the hint when she brought the beers and left us menus. "Just yell when y'all are ready."

Nick sat quietly, watching me figure out my approach. Hell, I thought. Sometimes there's nothing left but honesty.

I laid my I.D. out on the table. Nick picked it up, looked at it, and then looked at me.

"Holy shit," he said under his breath. He looked at me again, and shook his head, chuckling. "God, I mighta known. Nobody I know is ever normal; it's my curse in life."

He laughed some more for the next couple of minutes, and I took it on the chin—bravely, I thought. When he had run out of jokes, not all of them funny, I ordered another beer for us both and settled in to tell my story. When it was over, I told him why I was soliciting his help.

"I don't have the time to screw up, Nick. I need to find out what's going on with this piece of land and Mr. Maupin's son. Fast. I've got to expose Lukas, so he can't do any more harm. I've got to get a couple of boys back home. But I need someone like you to help me. You know people here; you know what's what. I want to go back into that bar tonight and find out some information I can run with. That means establishing a good rapport with the bartender on duty, wouldn't you say? Who hears more stories than you guys? Your help could make a real difference."

"Why me?" he asked. "Why not hire a local detective to help out?"

I was ready for this question. "Because until all the pieces fit together, I don't dare trust too many people. My cover's somewhat jeopardized by the incident with Mr. Davis at noon. Then I told Mr. Maupin and his housekeeper who I really am. It doesn't take long for these things to go haywire. I sensed something in you, Nick—I think you may be an honorable man, one who likes helping out however he can. Don't do it for me; do it for those innocent people who're getting screwed to the wall."

He let my words sink in for a few seconds. "I'm a sucker, that's what I am. This guy Lukas sounds like your worst nightmare, picking on teenagers and old men." He shook his head slowly. "That's not much of a human being."

I beckoned for our waitress. "Let's eat. We might be looking at a long night."

Nick raised his bottle to mine in a silent toast: partners.

He'd been wrong about one thing, but I kept it to myself. I was a team player, in my way. For years, I'd found happiness to be no more complicated than the steady pulsing of rhythm guitar, bass, and drums, holding down the bottom while the lead instruments could feel free and safe enough to soar over the steady groove we'd set. Ron's death had cut me off from all that. Sometimes a partnership was all I craved.

I could sense excitement in Nick also. Maybe he'd had

enough of observing the world from a neutral spot behind the bar. Our food arrived and we tore into it like a couple of hungry dogs.

We got to the Rosewood before the onslaught of eager swingers. It was still the dinner hour, so the restaurant was hopping, but the bar wouldn't crank up for a good couple of hours. Five people sat around nursing their drinks, waiting for the real night to begin.

"Maybe the smoke's not so thick this early," I mused, "but the air of desperation certainly is."

Nick shrugged. "Lil, you wouldn't make much of a bartender; this is nothing. Around closing time, people do some pretty strange things."

I didn't have much trouble believing that. "Speaking of bartenders, is your pal here?" It had turned out that Nick knew bartenders all over town.

Nick nodded toward the bar. "Yep. That's him working."

"And you're sure he's okay? He's a good friend? You can trust him to keep his mouth shut?"

"How do you know you can actually trust me, for that matter?"

I must've looked worried, because Nick said, "Ha! Gotcha! It's a little fault I have—I like to pull people's chains sometimes. C'mon, I'll introduce you."

The man behind the bar was in his late thirties, with sandy hair and a reddish mustache. He moved nicely enough to be a daily swimmer. When he saw who I was with, his face relaxed into a smile.

"Nicky! Good God, the world must be turning upside down—Nick Papalonis out in a bar?" He lowered his voice. "A ritzy singles bar, at that."

He smiled at me. "Joe Thacker," he said, as he offered his hand, "but my friends usually just call me Mr."

Nick rolled his eyes. "It's an old joke," he said.

I sat down at the bar. "I'm glad to meet you, believe it or not." I looked around me. "Got any Mexican beer?"

Joe served us cold Dos Equis and pulled up a stool on the other side of the bar. "Okay, Nick, hit it. You said over the phone you guys needed to pick my brain, so pick away. You never know when the place will suddenly fill up. I'm all yours while you got me."

Nick nodded at him once. "Okay, this is the deal. Lil here needs to know some stuff but we can't exactly tell you why yet. Can you live with that?"

"Man, I don't even wanna know why anymore. My brain is filled up with useless crap as it is."

I took the ball. "Joe, do you know anything about someone named Donald Lukas?" He shook his head. "How about John Maupin, Junior? Lives around Free Union, works around Charlottesville, I think."

Joe nodded. "Afraid so. The guy's all over the place, unfortunately. What do you need to know?"

"What's he into? Who does he hang around with? That sort of thing. I just want to get some kind of general picture."

"He's a little bit of a gadabout, actually. He owned part of a radio station once. That folded and he opened a business-supply place that did pretty well. Later on, he opened another store nearer to the university and added textbooks and stuff, and it's still going. I think he sold his part of it, though. I don't know what he's doing now."

Joe stopped talking and went to give the man at the end of the bar a drink. He was back in a flash.

"So what else can you tell me about the man? I've got a hunch there's a lot more you're not saying."

He snorted. "The man's a first-rate asshole. He's not what you'd call well liked."

"That's the impression I've gotten before. What's wrong with him?"

Joe shook his head again. "From what I've heard, he's not really thought of as a real member of the business community. He has family money, without much else going for him, so he's managed to stay afloat somehow. What can I say? The guy's a real jerk with a capital J. I've known people who've worked for him in the past. He has the personality of an irritable weasel. Sort of looks like one, too, now that I think of it."

Nick broke in. "Does he come here? Have you seen him in action close up?"

"Yeah, he's been in here." He lowered his voice. "Let's just say he's not too popular here."

"Why not?" I looked around the room. "He wouldn't be the only jerk to walk in the door, would he?"

Joe hesitated a moment. He looked like he was weighing something in his mind. Nick broke the silence.

"Man, what is it?"

"Okay, I'll tell you this, but I don't want it to get around where it came from. Bartenders need to be more discreet than most, you know."

I tried to look reassuring. He already trusted Nick, so he could only be worried about me.

Joe lowered his voice even more and leaned in toward us. "Maupin was in here one night during the winter. I remember the night because it was snowing when I came to work and it had a little sleet mixed in with it—definitely not a good night to be out. I figured I'd be here for the handful of stragglers who were foolish enough to go out, and wouldn't make much in tips. I was right.

"Maupin came in kind of late—I'd been thinking of closing up—anyway, he'd been drinking. I can usually tell right away. He ordered a triple, which I almost didn't serve him, but he insisted he was okay. It's really a fine line to walk, as a bartender. A customer goes into a bar for a drink, and that's what he should get; but the bartender is responsible for not giving liquor to someone who's too fucked up already. Anyway, I decided he was more worked up about something than actually stinking drunk, so I served him. Probably I shouldn't have." Joe looked a little defensive still.

"So what happened?"

Now the bartender was almost whispering. "He picked up a woman I know pretty well—she's a regular here. She's an okay person, but she's had bad luck with guys, one after another, from what I can tell. Anyway, I looked up and they were gone. I didn't think anything else about it, until I saw her a few nights later, wearing heavy makeup. You could see the bruises even through her Tammy Faye Bakker disguise."

"He beat her up?" I hadn't counted on this.

Joe nodded. "He sure did. I made her talk to me; I just felt bad about it. Apparently when they left here the lady thought they were going to her place, which would've meant going out on Twenty-nine North for three or four miles, and turning into one of the subdivisions out there. Anyway, Maupin didn't turn off where she told him to. When she started getting scared, he said he just wanted to pick up something to drink from some bootlegger he knew, so she didn't freak out right away.

"When they'd gone about ten miles out toward Ruckersville, she started getting these weird vibes that scared her pretty bad. She told him she'd changed her mind, and was tired enough to go back home and go to sleep. He slammed on the brakes—mind you, it was still sleeting a little—and nearly cracked up the car. Anyway, he went a little crazy and started hitting her. She said that the more frightened she got, the more excited he became."

The bartender stopped for a moment. "Is this helping? I don't like to spread shit like this around unless it's necessary. Gail was really telling me this in confidence."

"Believe me, Joe, this is information I badly need. So what happened? Did she get raped? How'd she get away?"

He smiled for the first time since he'd started the story. "She's got these long fingernails you wouldn't believe, and it's a good thing, as it turned out. She raked them across his face hard enough to draw blood. He was so surprised it made him hesitate for a split second. She jumped out of the car with her clothes half off and ran into the woods until he'd gunned the car back onto the road. She was half expecting him to follow her into the woods, but he didn't. She flagged down the next car. It was a couple from Gordonsville, trying to make it home in the storm. They turned around and took her home and stayed with her until it got light outside."

"Did she call the cops?" I asked.

"Nope." He shook his head. "She just wanted it to be over. Cops aren't always sympathetic to women who've gone along willingly. She figured they'd put her through more horseshit, and she was probably right. She's strong, I'll give her that; she called in sick for a couple of days and took Valium until she could get along without it. Then she went back to her life the best she could."

We were silent for a few minutes. It was a grim picture. I hated to think just how often things like that happened in the night, and how many of them went unreported.

Nick spoke first. "Has he come in here since? Wouldn't you want to tear his face off?"

"He hasn't shown his sorry face. I offered to do something about it, but the lady just wanted to forget it. She really thought he was gonna kill her. She said that while it was going on, a newspaper headline flashed in front of her. She could see herself dead, killed by a maniac no one would ever suspect. If he'd come in here he wouldn't have gotten as far as putting his butt on a barstool, I'll tell you that much."

Suddenly I felt like being somewhere with more light, myself. "So the guy's an asshole and a pervert, too."

"Yep, that he is. Gail said something that stuck in my mind. I can still hear her saying it. She said that she'd known guys who'd had too much to drink and got carried away by what they wanted—like I said, she's known a lot of guys, and a fair number of 'em have been losers. But she said Maupin was somehow different. He was into the violence. I mean, really into it. She got the feeling he was right at home there, if you know what I mean. A real sicko."

I stood up and plunked down some bills for the beer.

"Nah," he said, waving the money away. "Just use the info to hurt the guy."

I smiled at him. "You can count on it." I stuck a twenty into the tip jar just the same.

FIFTEEN

We stepped outside into cool spring. The first stars were just beginning to come out. We stood there for a few minutes, lost in our own separate thoughts. I thought so, at least, until I asked Nick my question.

"How many bartenders do you know?"

He smiled. "I thought you might get around to that. The answer is . . . hmm . . . six or seven current ones, and let's say a few more, maybe five or six, who're out of the business these days. You thinking what I'm thinking?"

I looked at his watch. It was still early enough to hit some bars before they became overwhelmingly busy. "Let's do it," I said.

In Virginia, the law doesn't allow bars to exist on their own without food being served, so even if a place is primarily a bar, it says RESTAURANT on the sign and serves a certain proportion of food. It was still the tail end of the dinner hour, so most bartenders wouldn't be that busy yet, we thought.

We made brief appearances in three places on Emmet Street, where Route 29 comes all the way into town. These bars were frequented by a mix of university fun-seekers and townspeople, leaning a little toward Mr. Jefferson's own. I met some interesting bartenders, but none who told me what I was looking for.

We moved downtown, hitting a couple of places that had bands setting up. At one of them a skinny, frizzy-haired guitarist somewhere around my age started warming up. For a minute I forgot about Lukas, John Junior, and the whole bloody mess. Nick noticed my reaction. "His name's Sonny. He's been in just about every band in town. The bands come and go, but Sonny, he gets any hotter and you won't be able to put out that fire."

"Who'd want to?" I mumbled. Anyone who thinks all the talent is in the big cities hasn't traveled around enough. I stood there, transfixed.

Nick glanced at the bar clock. "It's borderline, Lil; the crowds are starting to come in, but it's not bad yet. It's up to you—wanna try one more place? It's nearby, just a block up the hill."

"Sure, why not?" It would beat going back to the hotel, worrying about what step I needed to take tomorrow morning.

This place was old brick, with beautiful dark wood. It was long and narrow, with steep narrow stairs leading up to a room where forks and knives were still clinking. A woman with a punk hairdo sat just inside the entrance, behind a little table containing a cash box and a hand stamper. A cardboard sign told us the cover charge was five bucks. "Hi, Sally." Nick smiled, "Mind if we just go in to see Eric for a minute or two? If we decide to stay and hear the band I promise we'll come out to pay."

"No prob," she said. "Help yourselves. The band's still setting up, anyway." She lowered her voice a little. "The idiot drummer forgot his bass drum pedal and had to go back for it." She was still shaking her head when we walked past her.

Eric wasn't really busy yet, customer-wise, but he was certainly preparing for it. Gleaming glasses hung upside-down from their racks above his head, and neat stacks of clean ashtrays sat upon a clean white towel. He was just finishing with a tray of freshly cut limes, lemons, olives and cherries; another container filled with napkins, straws, and coasters showed off his organizational skills. They would come in handy, I knew, when the music was hot and the customers were thirsty and in a hurry. He'd started to fill a container with ice from the machine under the bar, when he noticed Nick.

"Hey, man, how ya doing? Haven't seen you in a while."

Nick shrugged, then shook his friend's hand warmly. "You know how it is. I've been busy doing nothin', I guess. Listen, man, I know you gotta keep working, but my friend Lil, here, and I need to pick your brain for a minute or two."

Eric looked around him, his eyes sweeping every square inch of space behind the bar. Apparently he was satisfied with what he saw. "Hell, I think I'm actually ready for once." He squirted some club soda into a glass and took a sip. "Want something? I can stop for a minute, I think."

Given my liquor consumption of the last couple of days, I thought a club soda might not be such a bad idea. Nick accepted a draft. We settled ourselves on bar stools, while Eric pulled one up for himself behind the bar. "Gotta rest the dogs, you know. I'm gonna be on my feet until after two A.M." He looked at me curiously. In Charlottesville you tend to see a lot of the same faces and mine wasn't registering.

Nick introduced me as an old friend, and I'll admit it was beginning to feel that way to me, too. Eric shook my hand politely. "What's up? What did you guys need to talk to me about?"

"We were wondering if you happen to know a guy named John Maupin. He's in his forties, probably late forties, and goes to the bars a lot."

Eric looked at me curiously again. "What you want with a scumbag like that?"

"So you do know him," I said evenly.

His handsome face turned ugly with feeling. "He comes in here, his ass is grass. He'd better not try it."

I looked at Nick, who looked back at me, and then to Eric. "What'd he do, man?" Nick asked. "It's hard to piss you off."

"The creep beat up a friend of mine, that's what." He looked at Nick. "You remember Patty, who used to hang out with the Reivers?"

Nick nodded and explained to me: "The Reivers were a great little band that played around town for a couple of years."

"So what happened?"

"Patty'd had a little too much one night and left with Maupin. She said she'd seen him around town a lot and thought he was okay. It was late—you know how it goes, she'd been downing shooters all night and let the wrong guy pick her up."

"Where'd they go? Didn't Patty live at the band house?" Nick asked.

Eric frowned. "Yeah, that's where she thought they'd go. Maupin said he knew a little place where they could get some more booze after hours, so they ended up riding around in the car instead. By the time they got out around Ruckersville, she'd sobered up enough to know she'd made a mistake."

My scalp tingled. He'd taken her out on 29 North, just as he'd taken Gail.

"How'd she get out of it?" Nick asked.

Eric looked embarrassed. He glanced up at me. I gave him a level look that said, I can take it if you can.

"Look, Patty's a real sweet person, but kinda casual about sex. We all were. Hell, this was before anybody outside the cities took AIDS seriously. She told me she thought she'd just jerk him off in the car, and she'd go home and forget about the whole thing. But when she tried to, uh, arouse his interest, he went crazy and started beating the shit out of her. The guy really went nuts, almost frothing at the mouth. She thought she was dead in the water."

"How'd she get away?" Nick and I asked this at almost the same time.

"They were near the intersection at Ruckersville, you know, where Route 33 crosses, going either left towards Stanardsville and the mountains, or right towards Barboursville and Gordonsville. That all-night truckstop is right around there on the left." We nodded, impatient to get to the rest of the story.

"Well, he'd swerved off the road when she came on to him so the car was at a funny angle, I guess. A couple of cars went by slow and one of them got the picture, apparently, because this big old Chevy truck pulls over and stops in front of Maupin's car. This huge dude from Greene County hauls ass out of his truck with a crowbar, and Maupin flings open the passenger door and throws

Patty out of the car and takes off like a bat out of hell. The big dude, who looks pretty scary himself, is all concerned and keeps saying to Patty to say the word and he'll find Maupin and kill 'im just like a dog. Patty's grateful as hell to this dude, but she just wants to get home to her own kind of friends. She ends up getting the guy to take her to the truckstop and wait with her until Corky shows up to take her home."

"Did she report it?" I had the feeling I already knew the answer. I was right.

Eric shook his head. "And tell the cops she'd been engaged in a sexual act in his car? No way. They wouldn't have done jack shit, except treat her like a whore."

There was something I didn't understand. "How could this stuff be happening around a town Charlottesville's size and the word not get out? The guy's been running businesses, for Christ's sake."

Nick had an answer I didn't really want to hear. "Suppose the other women *didn't* get away? After all, Gail didn't talk and Patty didn't talk. Maybe there were others who couldn't talk, not after Maupin got through with them."

A wave of nausea rushed through me. Could Maupin be a killer? Lukas was, and they had the land deal in common—that much I did know. Were they more connected than I had originally thought? Something else had struck me. What the hell was out 29 North? Was he trying to take these women someplace in particular? I was beginning to think so. But why?

I asked Eric one last question. "Whatever happened to Patty? Is she still in town?"

He shook his head. "That whole thing really freaked her out bad. The last I heard, she'd moved back to northern Virginia, where she had family. I heard she's stopped drinking."

I hoped so. I slipped Eric another of Jim's twenties before we left, and on the way out stuck a ten in Sally's cash box in support of the band, drummer and all.

The next morning, early, I patted the Mercedes good-bye for good and drove off in a beige Toyota. This time I wanted to blend in. I was through with Betsy Hunt and her ilk.

A brief phone call to Dora had told me what I needed to know right now: that John Maupin spent his work hours, as did his wife, at their newest business, a video-rental store up on West Main Street. We'd just see about that.

I walked into the store and browsed around for ten minutes or so. A few people came in to return rentals from the night before, but things weren't all that bustling. A harried-looking skinny blond woman walked around the store with a clipboard, checking this and that. I took her to be Sharon Maupin. This was confirmed when a young employee asked her to sign for an order that had just come in. She sighed and stopped what she was doing. The woman looked bone-tired, and it was only nine-fifteen in the morning.

There was no sign of John Maupin. There was a double-door setup going into a back room. The employee, probably a UVA student, kept going in there, so I assumed it was a supply area of some sort.

I looked around some more. Some steps to the back seemed to lead to a glassed-in room overlooking the store. That would be where the boss could look down and check on the comings and going of his customers and employees. Let's just see what would make you come down those stairs, I thought.

After Sharon had signed the papers and the delivery man had left I approached the counter. In my sweetest voice, I asked the young man for a film I'd already noticed they didn't have in stock, *A Murmur of the Heart,* an old one by Louis Malle. When he checked their listings and didn't find it, I insisted he look for it more thoroughly—I was sure I had seen it there before. Sharon heard the beginnings of a disturbance and came around to help out her employee. My voice rose in response. I loved playing to an audience.

When Sharon assured me for the umpteenth time that they did not have, and had never had, this movie, I started ranting and raving about provincial attitudes in the South. Meryl had nothing on my performance. I let my voice rise to fever pitch, yelling about anything that came to mind, from censorship in the arts, to Jerry Falwell–type attitudes, straight to some heartfelt sentiments about the popularity of Sylvester Stallone. All the while, I kept an eye peeled at the stairs to my left.

Sure enough, just when I had begun enjoying myself—I was giving a critical review of *Howard the Duck*—I heard footsteps hurrying toward us.

John Maupin was as bland-looking as they get, what I like to call perfectly beige. He was probably around five eleven, but a little thin and under-exercised. He looked soft. A lackluster brown mustache covered up an indistinct upper lip. The hair on his head was the same color, brownish-blond, and hung limply. He moved awkwardly, walking with his feet turned outward, slouching. He wore red pants, and I thought he should've known better. The gold chain around his neck didn't help. All in all, the man impressed me as someone who had never challenged himself one day in his life. It was hard to believe he was the son of the handsome old man I had talked to, although I'd already seen his photo. Right now a flush crept up his neck. He glared at me hostilely, repeatedly pulling at his mustache.

"What seems to be the trouble here?" he demanded.

I kept on going, in a near shriek. "The trouble is that you people have a taste for bologna when you could be eating the finest pâté de campagne. I'm ashamed to be seen in a place with such hideous taste in film. I'll bet you've never even heard of Jean-Luc Godard. How many Fellini masterpieces have you ever watched, sir? And let us not even mention the great American director John Cassavetes. I tell you, the bottom crust is on the top these days. The bottom crust," I muttered darkly.

His voice lowered to a hiss. "Yeah? And you can get your sorry ass out of my place of business before I throw you out." He then reached under the counter for something, but I didn't wait to see what it was. I'd found out what I wanted to know.

Outside, I settled down into the Toyota and hummed to myself a little, biting into the perfect honeybun I'd gotten earlier in a bakery up on Fourteenth Street. In reviewing my performance, I realized I'd started out as Meryl Streep and segued to Bette Davis halfway through. Hell, I thought, if I'd had more time I could have thrown in a little Joan Crawford, say from *Mildred Pierce*. All I'd needed to do was get a sense of how the guy vibed, so I could follow him to the gates of hell. The rest was pure pleasure.

The night before, I'd told Nick I could handle things from now on; he'd been of invaluable help, but he was an amateur, and I didn't want to risk his getting hurt. I hadn't said that, of course. I really was grateful for what Nick had done, and I hadn't wanted to step on his pride. I'd promised to keep him apprised of what happened next, and I'd meant it.

When I'd gotten back to my hotel room I'd called Lena and Joe in Texas. The boys were fine, helping Joe rebuild a motor for the pickup. Lena said that Eugene was looking a little healthier, even sitting in the sun a bit. He'd discovered a pile of Zane Greys in the trailer and drank iced tea most of the day, reading.

I'd told them the case was on the verge of breaking—I could feel it—so to be extra careful until I next got in touch. Another call to Jim and Ruth had been for the same purpose. Now I was free to sit and wait. Most things do rise to the surface if you wait long enough.

I spent the rest of the day sitting in the car, keeping an eye on the store. Maupin didn't come out until closing, with Sharon. I followed them to a restaurant at the edge of town, and then home. I waited just past the turnoff to the big house until it appeared no one was coming back out. Exhausted and badly in need of a good stretch, I went back to the hotel to sleep. I was back out at Free Union by six-thirty the next morning.

For three days, my routine hardly varied at all. I spent my days dogging Maupin wherever he went, and the man didn't go many places I was too interested in. This guy is too boring to be a crook, I thought.

The Toyota started resembling a Dempster Dumpster, from all the junk I collected and discarded in the backseat. Once while he was at lunch, I ran in desperation to Back-Alley Disk and picked up some new tapes. I had listened my old ones to death. Rickie Lee Jones, Mary Margaret O'Hara, the Cowboy Junkies, and Miles Davis did a lot to help my flagging spirits. Neil Young played some fine rock and roll, with all the heart left in it.

I must've shown up at the Blue Moon Diner a dozen times for

the best burgers and breakfast in town. The owner was the cook, and kept a jukebox that was as good as the food and the company. While keeping an eye on Maupin's store, I watched him grilling up huge mounds of home fries with peppers and plenty of onions. It was a detective's dream—I could do my boring stake-out and hear Elvis at the same time.

Who said work couldn't be fun?

On the fourth morning, there was a change of routine. Sharon hadn't been in the car with Maupin when he came into town. A day off? It was a variation in the routine, at least, and I was grateful for that much.

He stayed in the store throughout his usual lunchtime, but at two o'clock he came out the front door, twirling his keys. His step had a jauntiness I hadn't seen before, and he was whistling a tune as he headed for his car. I started up the Toyota and pulled out behind him. I was going to stick to this sucker like a tick to a dog.

Traffic was thick, as it seemed to be most of the time in C-ville these days, so it was easy to keep from being noticed. Maupin meandered about, stopping at the branch of the bank across from the university, then again for gas at the corner of University and Emmet Street. I hung back and parked in a bus stop while the attendant filled his tank and checked the oil. Lazy, too, I thought.

Just as a bus bore down upon me, he pulled out, headed north on Emmet. I waved at the driver and made the light, a half-block behind my prey.

He made one more stop, to pick up something to eat at a fast-food joint near the intersection of Barracks Road and Emmet. While he was waiting in line at the take-out window, I ran inside and grabbed a taco myself. I beat him out of there and waited at the driveway of the Chinese restaurant next door.

He headed past the shopping centers, past the turnoff to his father's property, out 29 North. My heart was beating fast. I was so eager I had to make myself hang back almost out of sight. He slowed down after the traffic began to thin out, probably enjoying the day, which was sunny and warm, a perfect spring gift. This time I wasn't playing tapes and I wasn't listening to WTJU—I was all concentration. My Walther was in the glove compartment, loaded, just in case.

Fifteen minutes on the highway took us to Ruckersville and the intersection where he'd stopped the car with Patty. He kept going north. Though 29 North could take you all the way into D.C., I had my doubts we would be going that far. At Madison he avoided the 29 bypass and headed west towards Brightwood. These little towns were more or less nestled in the foothills of the Blue Ridge—close enough to have a bear-hunting season. I had to hang back a lot more now, to keep from getting noticed.

Presently he turned off into a little side road, and I waited a minute before turning in after him. The road started out paved, then turned to chunky gravel that made the Toyota protest. I slipped into second, then first, and pressed on, even after ruts became the norm rather than the exception. There had been a house at the beginning of the turnoff, but the ones I saw now had long ago been abandoned. I wondered why the road was even as good as it was.

Now the road turned into not much more than a path, with weeds and rocks taking up where the gravel had stopped. I realized I was sweating as if I'd been for a long run. Bushes and briars were scraping against the car now and the fear of being discovered became a real concern.

I stopped and turned off the motor. I could hear a car laboring in the distance ahead of me, and then a motor being shut off. I heard a couple of car doors and some voices in the distance, though not close enough to make out what was said. Then there was the slamming of another door, followed by silence. I stood by my car for a long second or two, wondering what to do. Quickly I backed it up and drove it into the driveway of the last empty house I'd seen. There, out of sight of the road, I backed it into an overgrown field. Coming out on foot, I did my best to cover up the tire tracks closest to the road. It would have to do.

The Walther was a comforting presence. I don't like guns, except for .22 rifles used for killing tin cans, a leftover pleasure from my Southern childhood. The .22s were fun and safe, if used well.

Handguns were another matter, but in my line of work I'd feel careless in not having one for protection, for myself or others.

Sweat streaming down into my eyes, I walked quietly toward where I'd heard the last sounds. I heard a rustle to my right and reached for my gun before the sound had stopped. A blacksnake slithered out of sight. "Calm down," I told myself, "you're gonna give yourself a stroke." I took a couple of deep breaths and held them, concentrating on my out-breath. I was ready to go on.

Hugging the edge of the road, I peeked from behind a clump of bushes. Maupin's car stood in a little clearing alongside a new Jeep. Just beyond the cars was something that looked so out of place it almost didn't compute: a prefab building, the kind that make nifty garages. This one looked like a little warehouse.

I looked around. There was no one in sight, so I decided to check out the Jeep. There was nothing on the outside to tell me whose it was, so I opened the passenger door carefully, a little at a time, praying it had been greased recently. The little click it made when it opened wasn't loud enough for the people inside to hear, I was sure, but I knew I didn't have much time—anyone coming out of the building would see me first thing. I opened the glove compartment and received a surprise: The registration was in Donald Lukas's name.

Shit! What was a girl to do? I closed the car door and crept around to the far side of the building, out of sight, behind the place where they'd exit. These dudes weren't for messing with, that much I did know. I recognized Lukas's voice, and then John Maupin's—the whiny one. They appeared to be having an argument. I crept closer. There were no windows to help me out, so I stuck my ear against the corrugated steel. I heard Lukas's voice at once.

"I give you one lousy assignment and you don't come through. How the hell do you think that makes me look?"

I couldn't hear every word, but just enough to get the gist of it. Maupin whined about how it was was getting harder to find "the right ones." Lukas roared, in real anger: "You expect me to do everything?" Whatever words that followed next I couldn't under-

154

stand, and then the volume picked up, passion probably having a hand in it.

"You son-of-a-bitch, I wanted a finished product by the end of the month. If you're too chickenshit to do that for me, you're worse than a little fucking cockroach." Then I heard what sounded like blows.

Maupin, who sounded scared to death, even through the walls, pleaded for another chance: "I know where I can get one more. Let me do that, Donny. I know I can. Then let me do something else for a while, that's all. We wouldn't wanna get caught with all the stuff. Let me clear out what's left and we'll take a break for a few months, and let things cool down."

Lukas gave an enraged bellow: "No goddamned guts, Maupin! Forget it! I'm getting tired of you anyway."

With these words said, Lukas flung open the door, which bounced loudly off the side of the building, leaving me with a ringing ear. He slammed the Jeep into reverse and squealed the tires backing up. He must've taken the little road at racing speed, the noise was that loud. Maupin closed the door a couple of minutes later, and I heard the click of a padlock. I heard him sniffling as he got into his car.

Shit, I thought. Now I'll have to pick the lock.

I waited until he drove off, and then waited another good five minutes to make sure they'd both really gone, before coming out from my safe harbor myself. Luckily, my old boss in New Mexico knew a lot about picking locks and liked me pretty well. A simple padlock wasn't much of a challenge.

It was dark inside, so I left the door open. I hate to admit this to anyone, but I've always been a little leery of the dark. I looked around. The place was mostly bare, with just a few chairs and an old bed with a stained mattress taking up the end nearest the door. Curious.

The other end had machinery of some sort, but I couldn't see well enough, so I searched around until I found the light switch. When I turned back around, I realized that the machinery was lighting equipment and a large-screen TV set. "What the hell?" I said. A metal cabinet against the wall was also locked, but again not in any serious way. I was in it within a couple of minutes at the most.

What I saw didn't make much sense—stacks of videocassettes, light bulbs, and filters. Then I noticed something else that didn't make sense at first: a video camera with extra lenses. These guys were making movies. I'd been expecting cocaine or crack, but not this. I took a cassette out of the cabinet and popped it into the VCR. Then I sat down on a metal folding chair.

The movie that started was badly shot, badly focused, and crude, even for a first-year film major. I recognized the room I was sitting in, though, and the metal bed to my right. On it was a young woman, wearing not even pasties, and it was the look in her eyes that made sweat once again start trickling down my face. I watched as two men tied her arms to the headboard, then spread-eagled her legs to the foot of the bed. Although I was only able to see the men from the back, Maupin's awkward movements were unmistakable. As if in a dream, I saw him climb on top of her first, and push frantically into her; she was screaming in terror and pain. The other man was next.

Then the men got out their party toys. The next thing I knew I was watching something quite different from any porn I'd ever stumbled onto. As the cameras rolled, I realized that what I was seeing was a murder—a murder done with real relish, slowly, slowly, the men savoring their work. The woman was no longer screaming or moving, but still the men didn't stop. At the first thrust of the knife, I clicked the projector off and puked all over the floor. I ran all the way to the car and then scraped bottom all the way out to the highway.

I stopped at a gas station at Brightwood and shakily called 911. I described the location of the warehouse and gave the names of the two men I had seen there, then hung up before the dispatcher could ask me again who was calling. I drove off to Charlottesville almost as fast as the Toyota would go, and didn't slow down until I felt the safety of the traffic snarls I'd complained about so bitterly earlier in the day. My heart was still pounding wildly, as if it couldn't slow down out of its own volition.

I pulled off a second time and bought a Coke to get rid of the acrid taste in my mouth; then I sat in the car until my pulse had slowed down to something resembling normal. So this was what the whole case had been about—snuff films, where the woman involved in the sex was murdered on-screen. I'd read somewhere that the going price was from $10,000 to $15,000 apiece. At that price, who cared about two lousy deaths in a porn palace in Richmond, or a couple of boys and an old man who, admittedly, hadn't had much of a life? Who knew how many Pattys or Gails had disappeared off the face of the earth, out of innocent drunkenness or desperation or loneliness?

I felt a rage that blotted out everything in my life that I held dear or sacred. I hoped the state fried their asses, and I hoped they'd let them anticipate a while first. Honest to God I did, with all my heart.

SIXTEEN

The next few hours weren't anything I'd care to relive. Exhausted in body and spirit, I went back to my hotel room and took a long soak in a very hot tub. When dinnertime came around I ordered some munchies from room service and settled in on the bed with some good Jamaican weed from my emergency stash, and the remote control. I flipped from channel to channel, first checking the news to see whether my discovery was yet out of the bag. Nothing.

That night I watched TV to forget. I didn't like to drink as much as I'd been doing, and I didn't like to use pot as a daily crutch, but I still reserved the right to occasional relief, and relief was what I sought that night. The rules applied to normal days, and I hadn't had one of those lately. These were days when the earth itself must grieve for the stupid beasts who roamed over it, killing and maiming each other for pleasure, the way no four-legged animal had ever done or ever would do.

As it grew later and the night more still, I opened the window facing Preston Avenue. There wasn't much movement—just a few stragglers returning home from the bars, I imagined, and some others returning from their jobs on the night shifts in the textile mill or one of the hospitals. I spent some time envying them their simple, uncomplicated lives, even though I knew I was wrong. Everyone's life has a price to pay at one time or another, and those faceless, nameless people still out on the streets at this late hour had their own stories of heartache and pain. But—*Damn it,* I thought—my job was a hard one for someone who preferred to think the best of others.

I thought of the time when laying down a good rhythm track had been the hard part of my day. A siren sounded from the direction of Vinegar Hill and I watched as an ambulance raced by. After that came a car full of teenagers laughing drunkenly as their Ford careened around the corner, going toward McIntire Road, probably headed for the bypass. They sounded joyous, at least. I hoped that either they would be more careful, or some outside intelligence was looking out for them.

I shut the window. Screw it, I thought. This job is what you do now—it's as simple as that. Self-pity won't help anything. It certainly wouldn't help those women who'd already died for some man's profit. What I needed to do was to make sure that those particular men didn't harm anyone else.

I turned off the TV and lay quietly in the dark. I'd wait until tomorrow's newspaper came out to see if there was any mention of what I'd reported today. If there wasn't, I'd lay my license on the line and go directly to the cops. It was the least I could do for the woman I'd seen murdered on film that afternoon. The cops would be mad, all right—after all, I had broken and entered, and I wasn't licensed to work in Virginia—but I really had no choice if I wanted to go on living with my conscience.

I didn't think I'd be able to sleep, so I took out a book I'd been carrying around by Paul Bowles, *The Spider's House,* and started reading the familiar passages I'd loved for years. It wasn't a comforting book—it was quite the opposite, in fact—but his writing was just what I needed to elevate me from the deep hole I found myself in. I drifted off to sleep with the book on my chest, blessedly free of dreams this time.

* * *

I woke up at nine o'clock, just as tired as when I'd fallen asleep. I lay there, still, for a few minutes, remembering where I was, then turned over for another hour of sleep. At ten I felt a little better, but not a whole lot. I showered, then went down to the lobby for some breakfast. The paper wouldn't be out until the afternoon.

When it did come out, there was no mention of Lukas, Maupin, or the warehouse, and no mention of a frantic call from a woman who'd witnessed her horror secondhand. The paper was curiously free of any of the wretched facts I knew to be true. What had happened to the information I'd placed at the cops' feet?

Tomorrow I would call Gordon Black's office to see how much trouble I'd be in for failure to check in with the local cops. In some states, that failure alone could cost me my license.

I don't know what others do at similar times of stress, but this woman took her butt down to the community pool for a long, mindless swim. The water eased the tightness in my muscles, and made me feel at peace with at least one of the elements. Churning around in my mind, though, waiting to pop out at my first un-guarded moment, was my mantra: What happened, what happened, what happened? I practiced the deep, regular breathing of the swimmer or the Buddhist or the soldier on patrol, and eventually I entered the no-time I'd been aiming for. It wouldn't pay to panic. I'd give the story another day.

I holed up in the hotel room with Paul Bowles for company, and smoked a little and thought a lot about my options, should this suspense last much longer. What would I do if my ability to work as a detective were taken away from me? I knew I'd adapt and move on, but I wasn't ready for that to happen. I couldn't figure out why the cops hadn't jumped on the info I'd given them; surely they had. Exhausted from my own thoughts, I fell asleep early.

The next day when the paper came out, I bought one from the delivery person before he had a chance to open the coin-operated machine. I took it up to my room like a child stealing away with a forbidden candy bar. As soon as I closed my door I leaned against it and glanced down at the front page. What I saw made my legs feel weak under me. I sat down on the floor.

John Maupin had been found dead in a ditch in Madison County. He'd been spotted late yesterday afternoon by someone driving home from work, who'd noticed something red out of the corner of his eye. It had turned out to be a red shirt on John Maupin's body, and it had been red with blood. He appeared to have been killed by a shotgun blast to the chest. Police refused to comment on whether they had been looking for Maupin in connection with another case. The story went on to give a brief biography of the dead man, making much of his family's influence in the area. It went on to mention that his next of kin had been notified, and the reporter concluded by saying that anyone with any information relevant to the case was to contact a Lieutenant E. G. Jackson at once.

I sat there on the floor, stunned, until I could think clearly again. I placed a call to Gordon Black's office, but he wasn't in. Then I got up and headed over to the Fox's Den.

Nick was working, but one glance between us let me know that he'd already seen the newspaper. I sat at the bar and he brought me a cup of coffee and whispered, "Sit tight until I can talk, okay?"

I nodded yes, still shaken. I watched him scurrying about, and his presence was comforting enough that I let my thoughts wander, which is the way I think best. Lukas must've killed him—he'd been furious with Maupin, and Maupin had seemed unstable enough to have reached some kind of a breaking point, I supposed. There had certainly been no love lost. Had Maupin called Lukas and tried to weasel out of his deal with him? Or could a desperate Lukas have simply decided to cut his losses while he still could? If Maupin knew the cops were after him, he would've been panicky enough to try almost anything, and that "anything" had probably been what got him killed. Lukas had most likely found it easier to kill him than to shut him up, I imagined.

Well, now I truly had no choice but to go to Lieutenant Jackson with the information I had. Having this close a connection to a recent murder was definitely worse than the threat of losing my license would ever be. As I sipped the strong, bitter coffee, I flashed on my grandmother complaining of an occasional "sinking feeling." I wondered if this was what she'd meant; I doubted it, a great deal.

It turned out that Nick didn't know Lieutenant Jackson, but he knew the police reporter, which was almost as good. The newspaper's offices were close to the Fox's Den, and reporters had long used it as a place to blow off steam during the lunch hours. The reporter's name was Raymond Jenkins, and when he walked in, proud as a rooster in the henhouse, Nick nodded to me. He held up a finger in a way that meant "wait a minute." I waited.

Jenkins was a cocky-looking guy who was too short to ever take his successes for granted. He looked like one tough little bulldog. He'd have to be; cops are even more jaded than your average private detective on a bad day. Getting information out of those guys had to be like trying to pry an oyster apart with your bare hands.

The lunch rush over, Nick motioned Jenkins over to the bar. "Raymond, meet my friend Lil. She's a detective, and I have a feeling you're both working on the same case."

Jenkins appraised me openly. I must've passed the test, because he pulled up a stool next to me and ordered a sandwich and a draft. He looked sideways at me. "What case would that be?"

"John Maupin," I said glumly. The words had wanted to stick in my throat, but I figured I'd better practice them for later, when it mattered the most.

"What's your interest in this? You aren't local, or I'd already know you."

"I'm working out of Maine, actually. A case brought me back to town and it's turned out to be connected with Maupin, among other things."

Jenkins hooted loudly. I supposed that was meant for a laugh. "Maine? Where the fuck *is* Maine, anyway? Don't they have igloos and mukluks?"

I lowered my voice, hoping to encourage him to do the same. "Look, Jenkins, you can help me with the part about not being licensed in the state of Virginia and I'll give you an exclusive that'll burn the pages of this sorry little rag you call a newspaper. Jackson's likely to rip my ass off about this thing, otherwise. You must know him. Think about it. If you and I cooperate, you'll get a better story for less work, and I get to eventually go home to my igloo."

I got up off my stool. I had to pee. "Think about it while I'm gone."

When I got back to my seat a few minutes later Jenkins was still there, and there was a draft beer in place of my old, empty coffee cup. He'd thought about it. He was chomping down hungrily on a huge pastrami on rye. He waited until he'd swallowed a mouthful of sandwich and sipped a little beer before he spoke.

"Jackson's gonna be a big surprise, I think." A smirk accompanied this statement.

"Let me guess. He's six foot two and a mean-tempered son-of-a-bitch. He eats private detectives for snacks."

Jenkins laughed again. I wasn't sure if I liked it better when he smirked or when he tried to be jovial.

"Well . . ." He drew it out into a couple of syllables. "The part about six foot two isn't half bad. 'Mean-tempered's' pretty right on, too . . ."

I wondered briefly about picking him up by the lapels on his cheap suit and shaking him to see if the story'd come out any faster. He was enjoying himself a little too much.

"Jenkins, Jenkins," I said wearily. "You're gonna make this fun for yourself at my expense. I really don't mind that, as long as you come through for me. But there *is* the element of time, you know. While our asses are parked here on these stools, maybe some sharp young reporter is out there dogging your story. Maybe some hotshot right straight out of journalism school." Old-style reporters who've come up from the ranks hate journalism majors and give them as hard a time as possible, or used to. I was banking that they still did.

He stopped chewing for a minute. I could see I'd struck a nerve. "Jackson's a woman," he said. "She's a real big woman, who'd just as soon shoot you as look at you, but she keeps it under control. Not only that, she's a big *black* woman, from somewhere up toward Ivy. A local girl made good."

Now that was something. C-ville was the same, but also

C-ville had changed, at least a little. I remembered when you never saw a black face on the police force at all, and certainly not a woman's. She'd have to be tough to stick with it—I couldn't imagine all the good old boys were gone from the police force. This could go either way, I thought. She could be more sympathetic because Maupin and Lukas had committed crimes against women, or she could be incredibly by-the-book, worrying about who was looking over her shoulder. A wild card.

When the last customers paid their bills and walked out, Nick came over and sat down with us while we talked. I'd given Jenkins just enough information to let him know I knew more than he did, but I'd left a lot out. I needed leverage with him to ensure his continued cooperation.

"Okay," he said, apparently satisfied with what I'd given him so far. "I can introduce you to her, but you know I can't guarantee anything—you just never know with cops. She might like you better than she does me, though, so you have a good chance. You promise I'll get an exclusive on this? You promise in front of Nick here, who we both know is an honorable man?"

I shook his hand on it. Nick shook both our hands, in turn. "Okay," Jenkins said again. "Let me make a phone call. If she's at the station we could go right over." He disappeared into the back corner, where there were phones inside real wooden doors that shut tight.

Nick looked over at me, and I tried to read what I saw in his eyes. "It looks like Maupin's hurt his last woman," he said.

"One down, one to go," I replied.

Walking over to the police station, I realized that in spite of the possible consequences, I was feeling a lot better. Jenkins, with his sour, cynical reporter's persona, had been just what I'd needed to pull me out of the low mood I'd found myself in since the events of the day before. I'd always been the kind of little kid who'd nurse a baby bird back to health and sneak food to the strays dropped off in front of our house. It had taken a while to toughen myself up enough to deal with the hard sides of life, and usually I didn't regret it, because my core still wasn't much different. But seeing the

164

woman in the film had shaken me. It was my tough side that would be able to avenge this woman, and I'd been handed that part back in the guise of a short, irritable middle-aged reporter.

The police station was where I'd remembered it, on Market Street at the edge of downtown. Like most other buildings in that part of town, it was made of red brick, but it was of a more recent vintage than many of its neighbors.

The desk sergeant didn't pay much attention to Jenkins; he just shrugged when he was told Lieutenant Jackson was expecting us, as if to say "It's your funeral." But maybe I was just projecting.

Lieutenant Jackson's office was along the north side of the building, up some stairs, and through a cluttered room full of smoke and sweaty men. Jenkins knocked on a scarred door leading into a cubbyhole office. "Oh, it's you," she said to him, although she'd known we were coming right over.

Lieutenant Jackson was indeed impressive. Massive would be the word to describe her body—hard and strong enough to intimidate the drunkest redneck on a Friday night. Her face was hard-looking, too; she didn't look like she'd be much inclined to cut anyone a lot of slack. But her eyes were what interested me the most. They were steely, like the rest of her, but the intelligence in them was palpable. It had taken a very smart woman to buck the racial prejudices of her native county, to work her way up to the rank of police lieutenant. With her, I felt as though I might have an even chance.

Jenkins introduced us—he'd already told her over the phone that I knew some things about the Maupin case—and backed out the door once he finished his part of the deal. "Call me," he said.

She motioned to an uncomfortable-looking wooden chair in front of her desk, then sat down in her own chair, which groaned under her weight. She eyed me levelly for a minute, letting the silence build up.

Pure cop, I thought. I'd seen that approach before, and it usually worked. Sometimes I liked to play that game, to piss off whatever cop it was for the hell of it, but now was not the moment for that.

"Lieutenant Jackson, my name is Lillian Ritchie. I'm origi-

165

nally from this area, but have been living in Maine, where I'm licensed to work as a private investigator. I came here on a case and stumbled into more than I was planning on. I'd like to settle up."

She let the second hand drag on a bit, then said, "You'd like to save your sorry ass, you mean."

"That, too," I admitted.

She let some more time drag on, maybe a minute, maybe four days; I couldn't tell. In truth, I was a child of the sixties, who never felt entirely comfortable with cops. Only I'd learned to hide it well over the years.

"A couple of days ago a woman called in a 911, and that phone call led us to a very interesting place. That wouldn't have been you, would it?"

"That depends on whether you would have been grateful to such a concerned citizen, or merely concerned with certain state statutes involving P.I. licenses and matters of territory."

She sighed, long and hard. "Look, Ms. Ritchie, I've had very little sleep for two nights, and I need my eight hours, you know what I mean? Just tell me what you have to say and I'll decide after I've heard it what I'm gonna do with you. You can take it or leave it."

There was really no choice. I plunged in, leaving out nothing except who my client was and the whereabouts of Jesse, Greg, and Eugene. She sat still for a minute after I'd finished talking, and I could see her sharp mind putting things together in a way that made it nice and tidy to a cop. "You'd testify about Lukas's being at the warehouse with Maupin?"

I said I would. I didn't want Lukas walking for lack of evidence leading directly to him. "These women Maupin tried to take out there—you think they'd testify?"

I cleared my throat. "Well, I don't actually know the women personally, but under these circumstances I believe there are those who could get them to come forward."

Abruptly she stood up. "I want a Co-Cola." She said it in the Southern way I'd heard it all my life. "You want something?"

"Thanks, I could use one." I dug in my jeans pocket for change. "Forget it," she said. "I'll be right back."

166

She was gone for only a minute or two, and when she came back we drank in silence. "I don't suppose you let the police in Richmond know anything about what happened with the boys and the murders in the Fan."

"I was going to do that after I'd pieced it all together. I just hadn't managed to until two days ago, when I followed Maupin to Madison County." It was lame, I knew.

"Cut the shit, Ritchie." She leaned over toward me, across her desk, and I involuntarily jumped back a little before I caught myself. That seemed to amuse the lieutenant—I could see the trace of a smile before she turned her face back into its stony cop's mask.

"You're smart enough to report crimes of that magnitude to the police. You're protecting your client, I believe."

When I didn't confirm or deny, she went on. "That's why you private cops gripe my ass. You play by the rules only when it *suits* you, while we who risk our lives every day have to toe the line. We have years of training and experience. We're terribly overworked and underpaid. And yet you private cops run around us like you're the fox and we're the stupid farmer who can't keep 'em out of their chicken house. Well, we can very well stop you and others of your ilk."

It seemed like I was breaking into a sweat a lot these last few days. This woman had the legal right to throw the book at me, and she was capable of doing just that. I waited uneasily in my chair, rooted to it like it was going to rear up and buck me off if I relaxed even a little.

She let me chew on her words while she left the room once more. This time I didn't know if she was going to the john or calling in someone to put the cuffs on.

When she came back, she seemed to have made her mind up about something. She sat across from me again, and leaned her elbows on her desk. "Is your client dirty?"

I thought about that before I spoke. "No, he's not, but he's guilty of the sin of omission, I guess you'd call it. Lukas was an old friend and my client owed him, so he let something slide he shouldn't have. He's a good man, though, and if he's left alone, I can tell you unequivocally he'll never skirt the edges of the law again. Lukas made a victim of this man and his family, and exploited the man's trust in order to do his own dirty work."

She nodded. "I'll have to speak with the prosecutor, of course, but I believe he'll agree with me on most points." She leaned back in her chair and stretched her long legs. "I want this Lukas. I want him bad. But I also don't want you stirring up the waters in my town anymore, and I'd like your word on that."

I wanted to sigh with relief, but I kept it in for the time being.

"You cooperate with me and my people and I don't bring criminal charges against you for failing to comply with the laws of the State of Virginia. You let me be the one to tell you when Mr. Jenkins can print his story. Not a word until I tell you. Is that understood?"

I wanted to grovel at this woman's feet, but I kept sitting in my chair, riding that wild bronc until the buzzer sounded.

She stood up, towering over me. I took my cue and got to my feet. She surprised me by extending her hand. Her smile was as unexpected as the sun on a cold, wintry day. "Off the record, that wasn't such a bad job, Shamus, not bad at all."

She sat back down. I saw her look up at me out of the corner of my eye as I turned toward the door. "Oh, by the way, in Virginia, you out-of-state P.I.s only need to make a little courtesy call to keep us happy. So that's one law you weren't breaking."

Embarrassed, reassured, and smitten with admiration, I handed her my number at the hotel and hot-footed it out into the sweet, warm smell of spring.

I spent the rest of the afternoon sitting in the little park near Court Square, gazing absently at the statue of Stonewall Jackson. Overhead, a cardinal sang his plaintive, bluesy little song from the top of a large magnolia. His "chew-chew-chew" was sad and beautiful. Even if I knew enough about birds to realize he was most likely just singing for reasons of territory, that did little to diminish the thrill he gave this tired detective. I'd missed cardinals, living so far north.

I went back to the hotel and called Ruth and Jim. They needed to be informed about what was going on, and I figured they deserved some notice. It wouldn't take Lieutenant Jackson long to figure out who my client was—I was betting she had a good idea already—but if I convinced Jim to come forward first, the cops would be more inclined to believe in his innocence. I'd believed him when he said he hadn't done anything illegal since the deal that had gotten him the money to start his business with. True, that part wasn't a pretty story, but people could grow and change, and I'd already seen a lot in the man that was pretty damned good. And Ruth was his ace in the hole—a woman who, even out of love, wouldn't stay with a man who was sliding backward.

We talked for half an hour, a three-way call full of shock and outrage on both their parts—outrage at what Lukas had done, and outrage at what kind of money Lukas had probably been laundering through their business. "If the government doesn't take every cent I have, I'm going to start over, clean. I'll lose my license over this anyway, so maybe I should just get out first."

"You haven't done anything wrong, Jim, so don't take that as a foregone conclusion. The drug deal might have to come out, but again it might not. Wait a while to see what happens, is my advice. When this hits the papers it's gonna be rough for a bit, but things die down eventually—they always do. I can make sure the reporter here knows you had no idea what was going on with Lukas. I can make him promise to put that in the proper light. Meanwhile, find a lawyer you trust and tell him everything that's going on."

Ruth spoke next, her voice tense and tired. "What worries me the most right now is the whereabouts of Donny Lukas. Do you think he'd want to harm Jim or me? What about the boys?"

I was going to get to that. "Do you have anyone you could visit for a couple of days—someone whose address isn't known to Lukas?"

Her answer was immediate. "Yes. My sister lives down in Charlotte County, near the North Carolina border. She and her husband have a big old farmhouse with a lot of land attached. I'm sure she'd love us to come for a few days. We don't see her enough."

Jim broke in. "Don't I have to stick around to talk to the cops? Won't they think I'm running?"

Who would blame him, given all the shit piling up at his door? But he was right—the cops had better be in on his next move, or we could all be talking next from those little telephones with the glass partitions between them, in the state penitentiary.

"Okay, I've got it," I said. "You guys get yourselves to a nice hotel, with security, tonight. Stay there until I talk to Lieutenant Jackson tomorrow. My guess is that she'll have someone take your statement, then let you go on to Ruth's sister's for safety. Lukas is probably running, but you can't be sure of that." I suddenly had a thought. "Jim, you've served with this guy in extreme combat situations. How is he under fire? Does he hold up?"

Jim was silent for a bit, and I could only imagine the pictures flashing before him. "He holds up," he said simply.

That was what I'd figured. Ruth asked again if the boys were in danger. I thought about that. "My guess is that he's got bigger fish to fry right now, though it's true that they're important witnesses against him. On the other hand, he doesn't have any reason to believe the cops know about him yet. Probably Maupin just threatened to tell the cops—he certainly doesn't know I saw him with Maupin or that the police know about his various connections. He's probably lying low, waiting to see what happens. As an extra precaution, though, I'll see if my friends could take the boys on a little trip or something for a few days."

Ruth said softly, "I miss my Jess so much. We're good friends."

I could see how. "It's just for a little longer, Ruth, then you can get on with your lives. Not many things are this bad."

"No, I guess they aren't." Jim stayed quiet on the line.

"Jesse will be back before baseball season even starts. Things will work out." I said it on faith, knowing all too well how some pain could linger.

Ten minutes later they called me back with the phone number and name of the hotel they'd call home for the next night or two. Jim gave me permission to tell the cops whatever they needed to know—a small, but important step toward becoming the kind of man he'd been telling the community he was ever since he got home from the jungle.

Nick called at six to see if I could use a burger and a salad in the friendly atmosphere of Random Row. It was the second best offer I'd had all day.

The next couple of days were nerve-racking in their slowness. There was action going on, but none I dared get into for now. I'd called Texas, where things hadn't changed much. Lena and Joe liked the idea of taking the boys and Eugene on a little jaunt, paid for by Jim. They had wanted to see some relatives in Gonzales, and this would be a good excuse. Jim's money would make up for the time off work.

Lieutenant Jackson called me in a couple of times to clarify what I'd already told her. The second visit was with the prosecutor, who wanted to know more about Jim's and Lukas's relationship, and assurances that what I'd said was the truth. He and the prosecutor in Richmond made a trade: Jim's testimony and signed statement in return for freedom from more embarrassing questions. They couldn't speak for the IRS, though. Who could? Even the authorities agreed that the boys were safer out of the state for the time being, though they'd need to testify when the time came.

Lukas still couldn't be found. Nothing had hit the papers yet, a fact that Jenkins reminded me of about three times a day. We were waiting for Lieutenant Jackson's okay, and it hadn't come.

On the third day, the call came. "You and Jenkins get down to my office as soon as you can. Maybe we can use the press to flush out this piece of slime."

The story ran, all right, with a large photograph of Lukas in his white suit, taken at a charity function in Richmond sometime during the past year. He was looking dapper, his arm draped casually around the shoulder of a beautiful woman who didn't look a day over twenty-one. The headline read, DEVELOPER SOUGHT IN MAUPIN KILLING. A subheadline ran above a photo of Maupin, saying "Link With Bizarre Porno Murders?"

It looked as if I'd be going back to Texas before I'd expected.

I hung around C-ville a couple more days, waiting for Lukas to surface. With the kind of publicity he'd been getting I figured the guy couldn't go out for a pack of cigarettes without someone spotting him. Jim and Ruth were safely nestled in the arms of Ruth's family down in Charlotte County. I'd spoken to them a couple of times and they'd seemed solid, capable of navigating this particular stretch of bad road just fine.

Lena and Joe were enjoying their little vacation with the boys and Eugene.

On Friday I asked Lieutenant Jackson if she needed me to stick around town any longer; I was anxious to get on with things. Promising to stay available, I decided to go back to Texas to wait for the word of Lukas's capture. The national press had picked up Jenkins's story, so I knew I could follow it in the *Austin-American Statesman* or the *San Antonio Light*. I wanted to be near a good party town when this sorry case was laid to rest. I needed to be where the beer was cold, the spices were hot, and the music was loud. I could wait in Lena's and Joe's house as well as I could in a hotel room in C-ville. But I had one more thing to see to first.

Mr. Maupin had lost some more ground in the days since I'd seen him. He was sitting up this time, but his posture just served to emphasize the emaciation of his body, which couldn't last a lot longer. I sat close to him, so that very little of his effort was needed for the mechanics of conversation. The content was something I couldn't do much about.

"Mr. Maupin, I've spoken to an attorney friend, who is willing to help you get your land back, and into the trust you mentioned. Under the circumstances, he could get some paperwork out to you within a day or two, if this is still what you wish to do. It's entirely up to you, though—I know you must have a lot on your mind."

A ghost of a smile flickered across his face. "I'd be most grateful for that help, most grateful. That particular wish hasn't changed."

"Good. Gordon's a fine man and he'll do well by you. He's also a history buff, so he said it would be a pleasure."

The old man nodded his head. "That's good. Thank you."

I felt there was something else I should say to him. I wanted

172

to be able to heal him with my words, but I knew they didn't have that kind of power—no one's could. We sat in silence for a few minutes, listening to the ticking of the old grandfather clock that took up the space between the two windows that looked out onto the side yard.

Mr. Maupin's voice broke the silence, its power startling me. "Why did he do it?"

I didn't have an answer.

"Rebecca and I had a wonderful marriage for almost fifty years. I never cheated on that woman once, although the opportunity certainly arose. I simply didn't want to. I loved my wife. I'd sowed my wild oats before marrying. John Junior grew up in a happy home. What could've made him do these terrible things to young, helpless women?"

I sighed. "I don't know, Mr. Maupin. I guess you could look upon it as some kind of sickness. He probably couldn't control a part of himself. Maybe he tried, though." I tried to sound hopeful.

"Sharon doesn't want to talk to me about him. I can sense she wants to spare my feelings, and I can also sense she's relieved he's gone. I don't even hate her for that. If his own wife is relieved he's dead—" He broke off, unable to continue.

"She'll talk to you when she can. She probably has a great deal to sort out first." I could but imagine.

"Did you find out what they were going to do with my land?"

"Not yet, but I expect we'll find out when Lukas is caught."

We let some silence pass between us for the second time. This time I broke it. "Mr. Maupin, I feel responsible for your son's death, in part. My investigation certainly made things come to a head faster than they would've, probably. I just want to say to you that I'm so sorry; I know he was your only son."

His bony hand touched mine, briefly. "I don't blame you, Miss Ritchie. I'm too old and sick to attach much importance to blame and judgment anymore. What's done is done. The rest is up to whoever is in charge."

I turned around to look at the handsome old man one last time before finally leaving the room. I knew I wouldn't be seeing him again.

My last day in Charlottesville went quietly enough. I had a drink with Jenkins, who was riding high. He'd had a front-page byline every day since the story ran, and now the AP wires had picked his stories up. We both knew there was a good chance that someone from the *Washington Post* would be giving him a call before long—every reporter's dream, about to be realized. I had to give him credit: He'd done some good writing, and he'd stuck to the agreements we'd made in private. My name was kept out of the paper—he'd only mentioned a certain "private detective who uncovered some evidence that led to the police investigation," blah, blah. I knew it was enough for Lukas to figure out who had fingered him, but I also figured Lukas had about all that he could handle for now. I was the least of his troubles.

Nick and I had a final dinner at Random Row. Some friends of his showed up and we scooted over to make room for them in the booth. It reminded me of the old days in C-ville, when the complications of life hadn't yet set in. I couldn't say I didn't miss those times, but I'm also a creature of the present. I knew it was time to move on.

In the morning I turned in the Toyota and took a shuttle to D.C. From there it was only a couple of hours to Austin. I slept all the way.

SEVENTEEN

Something always happens to me in Austin; it's as if a chemical change comes over my very blood, making me feel both totally relaxed and revved up to the limits. It's a city known for being laid back, but a part of me also shoots straight into overdrive there. Maybe that's one reason it's a great party town.

I decided to spend the day nosing around some of my favorite haunts. This time I rented a brown Toyota Camry near the airport, and drove over to the first Popeye's I saw for some of the best so-called fast food in the world: spicy Cajun-style fried chicken with a side of red beans and rice. The huge iced tea was the perfect foil for the heat that was starting to build up even this early in the season. Austin springs are cool only by comparison with her summers. I'd had to shed a layer of clothes already.

No one was expecting me. Lena and Joe would be gone for another day or two, and I hadn't let Robert know I was coming back so soon. Some quiet contemplation could only help restore my tired soul. I headed west to Lamar, then took the long way around, heading south until Enfield, then looping across Mopac Boulevard to West Thirty-fifth Street. I was looking forward to an afternoon at my all-time favorite resting spot.

Laguna Gloria is a large old Italianate villa that serves as the foremost art museum in Austin. Its twenty-nine acres are nestled in a little cove on the Colorado River, where it's been dammed up to make Lake Austin. Its name translates as "Glory Lagoon," and it's that, all right, and more—a place where some of the most beautiful, large live-oaks in the state of Texas coexist comfortably with tall palm trees that remind us of the close proximity of the tropics. For many years, a few walking trails have been there for the public to enjoy, with palms growing along the riverbanks in some spots, cypresses in others. There are places along the trail where it's possible to believe you're in the middle of a lush bamboo forest, rather than in a town that's grown to nearly a half-million in the last few years.

There weren't many cars there, so I assumed the museum was between shows. I bought a can of juice from the dispenser outside and sat down on a bench underneath the biggest live oak, an old grandmother tree at the east end of the building. The air smelled great, with something spicy I couldn't identify. I remembered a time when huge wind chimes had hung from the very branch I was sitting beneath now. I knew that along the trails other sculptures that I'd enjoyed in past years would have been replaced by now with new works of art that would be just as delightful. It was that kind of place.

I walked to the other side of the building, closer to the water. There, I looked down at a natural amphitheater, where musical events and plays often accompanied art openings and the like. It was simply done. The hillside was terraced, and some steps had been added along the edges, to make the descent easier. At the bottom of the hill, a little area had been covered with concrete to make a simple stage. Several tall palms stood sentry over the sleepy-looking river, and the combination gave the place the look of a tropical paradise; maybe it was. My heart picked up its pace.

I lay down on the ground near the top of the hill and looked up at the bright blue sky through the trees that sheltered me from the heat of the sun. I laughed out loud when I realized there were several sharp objects sticking into the back parts of me. So this was, after all, Texas, where things tend to be prickly. That was fine by me—it kept them from getting too sentimental and sloppy.

I fell asleep like that for an hour or so, then walked along the trail, stopping a couple of times to sit by the water and practice the art of not thinking.

I left the car where it was and walked next door to Mayfield Park, to see if the peacocks still roosted in the live oaks there, and to see if they still ruled the grounds of the old estate someone had been generous enough to leave to the city. Their shrill cries greeted me welcome. About a dozen of them lounged casually in the treetops, while a few roamed around the property, giving lucky visitors a glimpse of the kind of beauty humans can only try to achieve, and never really do. It was an afternoon I'd pictured many times in my mind's eye during the frozen Maine winters.

This time when I drove off I headed over to another favorite place on the river. Austinites have long enjoyed a series of hike and bike trails that follow the river for miles, going from deserted, quiet spots to popular gathering places for joggers wearing all the latest apparel. I exited off South Lamar and found what I was looking for. An elderly black woman was fishing, near a little family of mallards that were flashing their green badges of color with pride.

I sat on a rock nearby, not wanting to invade the woman's peace, but enjoying the quiet way she went about her pastime. I knew there were some older people who'd been fishing the river in these spots since they were kids, certainly before the city showed much interest one way or another. Her equipment was simple, a bamboo pole, with worms for bait. The cork bobbed briefly, and I watched her pull in a little sunfish. She carefully removed the hook from its mouth and gently dropped it back into the water. She looked over at me and smiled. "He's just a baby. I don't guess I'm that hungry for a fish fry after all."

I smiled back. "Catching much today?"

"Nah," she said. "I just like to fish. My daughter drops me off on her way to work, and I spend my time halfway fishing, halfway watching those pretty ducks over there."

I could see why. Maybe before I left town I'd stop by some morning with a bucket of worms and join her.

After a while, the old woman packed up her things and left with her daughter, who'd waved at her from the car. "Maybe I'll see you again," she said, turning toward me. "You like to fish?"

"I used to," I admitted.

"You'll remember how," she said. She walked off slowly, a little stooped, the way people move when age has settled into their joints. By the time she reached the car, she'd picked up a little speed, but just a little.

I sat there on the riverbank until the traffic thickened on the bridges and the sound of car horns and the smell of exhaust told me it was time to wrap it up for the day.

I wasn't through, though. Dodging traffic as much as possible, I drove around the section of town known as Clarksville, one of my favorite areas. Clarksville had been a black section in Austin's early days, but eventually a few hippies had moved in, followed by a little bit of everybody else. It had been a fun neighborhood when I'd lived there before. There had been an honest-to-God ice cream parlor, and Nau's Drugstore, where breakfast could be had for way under two bucks, still stood. When I'd lived there before, a few streets were still unpaved, and more than one old person could be engaged in a conversation that could last all afternoon. There were signs of gentrification now, and I wondered if there was still the odd good deal on a rental house with a pecan tree in the backyard.

I passed my time this way, visiting here and there. I passed by the Treaty Oak, which looked sick, all right. I hoped the people who'd sworn the old tree had some life left in it were right, in spite of the way things looked.

I drove past the Deep Eddy Cabaret, where I used to play pinball with my friend Dinah. The natural swimming pool behind it wasn't officially open yet, but I wondered if kids still climbed over the fences on hot nights. It was too early for the cottonwoods that loomed over it to shed their fluff into the water, though at the right time of the year that was part of what you put up with to swim there. This area, too, hugged the Colorado, all a part of the River City.

Another brief drive took me into south Austin. The little streets there were narrow, with small houses and lots of trees, and houseplants hanging on the porches. This was working-class, mostly, with Chicanos and old hippies in some neighborhoods, and whites in others. I drove past the site of old Armadillo World Headquarters, which had been *the* alternative-music club in the late sixties until the mid-eighties, when it was finally bulldozed to make room for yet another skyscraper. I smiled to myself when I saw the new building looking mostly empty; somehow, things had never worked out on that particular site. Call it the Texas oil crisis, or call it karma, but it looked lonely to me. I wondered whose hex had been the one to work.

When the sun started going down and I felt hungry, I headed up North Lamar to Threadgill's, where the style of food was Texas country cooking, the way you wished your mama still cooked it. It was a little before six, and Shiner longnecks still went for a quarter for the remainder of happy hour, which they called Howdy Time.

It was Wednesday, so Jimmy Gilmore would be playing that night until eleven or so. Wednesday nights at Threadgill's went back to the forties, when Kenneth Threadgill, a blues yodeler in the Jimmie Rodgers tradition, started having friends over to play for each other. The place had been an old gas station at the time.

In the sixties, Janis Joplin had been a young misfit in town, and the old man had taken her under his wing, encouraging her to use her powerful voice the way it felt right. The place had burned down since then, and Kenneth Threadgill was gone, but one of the original owners of the Armadillo had built it back, turning it into a boisterous, friendly place with a roadhouse feel. Jimmy Gilmore, a heaven-sent Texas singer and songwriter, had taken up the Wednesday night tradition, playing with his own band and whatever friends showed up.

That night I had a vegetable plate, with some of the most delicious cornbread I'd ever eaten. Afterward, I settled in to listen to the music, happily following the lyrics Gilmore sang in his plaintive West Texas style. I didn't know a soul in the place, but it didn't matter—I was pulled into more than one great conversation that night. It did my heart good to realize that Austin still had a loose feel to it, skyscrapers and yuppies be damned.

179

I drove out of Austin toward Lena's and Joe's late that night, relaxed and without a care in my heart. I'd left the depravity of Lukas and Maupin behind in Virginia, where it could be laid to rest by someone other than me. I'd already done my part. Now I'd just wait it out for a few days and take the boys home when I got the signal from Lieutenant Jackson.

It's simple now, I thought. It's really over.

And that was my first bad mistake.

EIGHTEEN

The house was pitch dark when I pulled up into the driveway, and I felt a moment's apprehension when I remembered I didn't even have a flashlight. But that was being silly, I knew—the events of the last few days were just getting to me. I got out of the car and took the key out from under the tub of flowers on the porch, as usual, hoping that no scorpion or snake objected in any serious way. In Texas, you've got to watch where you put your hands.

It's a funny thing about houses without their owners. You see a place filled with people you care about time after time, and then you see it empty and it's just another lonely box with four walls. I turned on some lights and the TV and went in to make a cup of tea before bed. A few minutes later found me settled in on the couch, with a light blanket and a pillow. David Letterman's band was rocking out as usual. Sid McGinnis played a blistering lead for a few seconds only before the commercial cut him off. I wondered briefly how it felt to play for that many people every night, realizing I'd never find out. With that depressing thought, I drifted off into sleep.

The sound of rain woke me sometime during the night. I got

up groggily and lowered the windows some, glancing out into the night. If this kept up, flash flooding would be a real possibility by morning. The caliche and limestone combination of the hill country doesn't absorb water easily, and sudden downpours always hold a certain amount of danger. Joe's and Lena's house sat up on a little knoll, and I thanked the spirit of Lena's ancestor, who had been blessed with such foresight. Then I fell asleep again with the lights still on.

I woke up again just after dawn, a victim of restless dreams. I tried for a couple more hours of sleep, then gave up and put on a pot of coffee. This was just going to be one of those days I wasn't completely awake for, and the weather didn't look like it was going to be much help. The rain was still coming down relentlessly, and the sky was as dark as my morning mood. I'd keep an eye out for that sky—it was just the kind that could turn the sick shade of green that meant Texas tornado.

I turned on the radio in the kitchen, to listen for the storm warnings I was sure to hear. I picked up a New Braunfels station, and sure enough the announcer was busy giving the latest information about conditions on the Guadalupe. A river rat's delight, the Guadalupe can be a powerful force when it's picked up extra water fast. There are low-water dams that release water on a regular basis, usually not in great amounts, but if the water level is already high, and it's raining hard, I knew the amount released could go from a normal two hundred cubic feet per second all the way to three thousand, making one hell of a raging river. Rafters and canoeists needed this vital information, and the stations faithfully kept them informed of the exact times water would be released. I listened with half an ear while the announcer repeated the times every few minutes. The water was high, and people were advised to stay off the river.

I drank a couple of cups of black coffee and followed them with some huevos rancheros and beans, my favorite breakfast in the world. One final cup and I'd have to decide how I was going to spend my day. I supposed I should call Lena and Joe, but only to let them know I was back. I doubted they'd travel in this kind of weather; most likely they'd be glued to the radio like me, checking for flash-flood warnings, along with most other south-central Texans.

A delicious thought crossed my mind: Suppose I didn't do a damned thing this miserable day but hunker down with a good book and a few cups of tea? In the little limestone house I had a new novel I'd wanted to get to earlier, *River Song* by Craig Lesley, about some Nez Percé Indians in Oregon. His first book, *Winterkill,* had been a delight and I'd waited impatiently for its sequel. I rubbed my hands together rapidly. Okay, I thought, the hell with the weather. Now, like Rhett Butler, I didn't give a damn.

I pulled on a slicker of Joe's before running out the back door. Even so, a few drops of water had found their way down my back by the time I'd reached the little house. My things were just as I'd left them, but neater if anything. Lena couldn't help herself, I thought—she was a neatnik, the way I was a slobette.

I grabbed the book and turned around, ready to fling open the screen door. What I saw made me drop the book on my foot instead. Lukas stood there in the doorway, the .38 revolver in his hand trained upon me. He was soaking wet, but he was smiling.

My heart pounded so wildly in my ears, it was the only sound I was aware of hearing for what seemed like the longest time. I looked around in desperation for something—anything—to help me out of the mess I was in, and found only a near-empty room next to a house with no one in it.

"What's the matter, bitch—cat got your tongue?" The smile on his face grew a little larger as my obvious panic registered in his bully's psyche.

"How'd you get here?" I stammered. "How'd you know where I was?"

He laughed, a nasty sound. "You think you're such a hotshot I couldn't follow you, bitch? Lying around some damned park, for chrissakes!"

Keep him talking, I thought. "Yeah, but how'd you get to Texas?" My voice sounded like that of someone on her last legs, which was how I was beginning to see myself. I'd have to work on that, if I lived long enough.

He snorted in contempt. "My man followed you to the airport in Charlottesville, got your flight number. I was on your flight out of D.C., nothing to it. I wore some old wire-rims and dressed down, that's all—that and the beard. The cops were looking for a natty dresser."

"Oh yeah? Where'd you sit on the plane?"

Why was I challenging this man who already hated my guts? It must've been some perversion of the fight-or-flight instinct. I needn't have worried, though. Lukas was in too good a mood to have me spoil it.

"I sat three rows behind you. I even went by you once on my way to the john. You were sleeping like a little baby."

Lukas came all the way into the room and looked around disdainfully. "So this must be where you stashed the brats and the old man," he mused. "Where are they now?"

My thoughts raced. Should I say they'd be coming back shortly, hoping he'd spare me for a while, or say that they were someplace else and I could lead him there? He'd still need to eliminate those witnesses, even if he was able to get rid of me. Greg and Jesse could tie him directly to the murders in Richmond. Without me, there'd be no eyewitness to tie him in with Maupin at the warehouse near Charlottesville. It was a toss-up at best. He'd want all of us dead. What the hell, I thought. Don't make it easy on him. He'll kill you anyway.

"The boys aren't here, and they won't be for a while. You won't be able to get me *and* them, Lukas. The corpses are starting to pile up. You're starting to trip all over yourself."

His face changed, and I could see the flush that crept up his collar. This man was used to getting his way. If I was going to die, the least I could do was to annoy him first.

He poked the gun into my stomach, just a little north of my belly button. The metal felt icy even through my clothes. A wave of fear came over me, so strong my knees started to buckle. Lukas grabbed at me with his left hand, digging in with the .38 in his right. "Don't try that female fainting shit on me, or I'll kill you now instead of in a while."

Call me an optimist, I guess, but that gave me a little hope. If Lukas wasn't killing me right away, I might have a chance to get away. I'd have to keep the paralyzing fear down, though, in order to be ready if an opportunity came knocking.

"Why'd you wait so long to do this? I was by myself in the house all night, you know." Even as I spoke, I realized he hadn't known for sure; Joe's truck was outside. That was why he'd waited.

"It pays to be careful," he said now. "I wouldn't want to walk in on a whole pile of cowboys, now would I?"

I could see another expression flash across his face, and it suddenly looked like boredom. Damn, the man was mercurial.

"Okay, *Ms.* Ritchie," he sneered, "enough of this shit. We're going to the car. You're gonna drive me to wherever you have those boys, or I'll just splatter you all over these nice rock walls."

That was an image I didn't care to entertain. "Couldn't I just go into the big house for a minute and get some dry shoes?" It was lame, but it was the best I could come up with. Maybe once inside, I could get to my Walther.

He snorted out another laugh. "And give you a chance to bring this along?" He pulled my gun out of his jacket pocket. I felt my hopes land somewhere around my feet. "Stop your stalling." He jabbed me again with his gun. I started walking.

We got into Lukas's car, a Dodge Aries rental. He'd come down a little since the black limousine the boys had seen him driving in that Richmond alley. He pushed me into the car, behind the wheel, while he got in on the passenger side. I put both hands on the wheel, which felt familiar and comforting, while he clutched the gun that had a bullet with my name on it.

"I'm asking one last time. Where are those boys? Otherwise, I'll just do you on the side of the road. I wouldn't mind all that much, you know."

A plan began to form inside my head, like a little miracle of life. It was extremely chancy, but it was probably the only chance I had. "They're in a cave on the river, one I used to like to explore. You'd never find it without me."

"Don't count on that. Drive. You fuck around with me, and your last breath will be a painful one."

I started the car. A little voice seemed to speak to me, from my years of experience; it said, "Keep him talking—it won't hurt." Why not, I thought?

"Lukas, tell me this: What were you financing with the money from those movies? Your business with Jim looked pretty good—there had to be something more to it."

He smiled. If I was guessing right, he was a man who enjoyed his little secrets; he liked feeling superior to those who didn't have such plans in the works.

I was right. "I don't guess it matters what I tell you now. You won't live to repeat it anyway."

"So spill the beans, Lukas. I'm all ears. I can take your little secrets to my grave." I crossed my fingers as I said this; there wasn't any use in tempting fate.

We'd reached our turn. "Now where are we going?" he growled.

"We'll stay on this for another ten miles, before we take a left."

"This had better be for real, Ritchie. Fuck with me, you pay with your life." A note of hilarity crept into his voice. "Of course, you're gonna pay with your life anyway. This'd just be a little sooner."

I didn't like the turn the conversation had taken. "So tell me, what was the deal?" I kept one eye on the road, and one eye on the gun, in case it should waver.

"Why not?" he said. "What do you know about pari-mutuel betting?"

I shrugged. "Nothing. It's something people do at race-tracks."

He shook his head sadly. "Ritchie, I'm disappointed in you. You don't know as much as I thought you knew. I was this close"—he held his thumb and index finger a couple of inches apart—"this close to getting pari-mutuel betting in Albemarle County." He turned a bit to face me now, his face a mixture of pride and rage. "In Virginia there needs to be a referendum in each place that's considering pari-mutuel betting. I had a lobbyist in my hip pocket. I had a piece of land all picked out. Then you had to go and stir up the waters." His face now was a study in pure hatred.

So he blamed me for all his troubles. That was why he'd gone to all this trouble to track me down and silence me.

"Mr. Maupin's land," I mumbled. "I get it now. Was that why you were in business with his son? Was it purely for the land connection?"

He shook his head. "Maupin was a loser who used to come to Richmond to find his little movies. He was so desperate for them that one of the guys who worked for me thought he might like to be a little more involved in the making of the films. He was an easy mark." Again his voice drooled contempt. "Maupin was a sicko who happened to come from a blue-blood family. I could use him any way I wanted. The land deal was just something I stumbled into."

I was all ears. "How did that happen?"

"Maupin's job was to find the girls and get them out to the warehouse. I thought he could handle it, but he was strung a little too tight, I guess. A couple of girls got away before he could get them out there. That was a major fuck-up, of course. All anyone had to do was figure out a pattern to what he was doing—say, a cop who got the story from a couple of different girls. So I had to take him off that assignment temporarily."

I was beginning to get it. "Let me guess, here. You had films of him and the other girls, though. You had proof that he was in on the killing of these women on camera. You made him sign that piece of land over to you—his family land."

Lukas glared at me. "You're not so stupid. That's exactly what happened. One thing, though—the guy could go out and rape and kill a few bimbos, but he balked at the idea of signing his old man's land over to me. Can you imagine that?"

I thought I could, and I hoped I lived long enough to tell Mr. Maupin a censored version of that very thing.

Lukas droned on now, though, enjoying his cleverness. "It would've made a great racetrack: two hours from D.C. by car, a few minutes by plane. There're plans to put in more frequent shuttles, you know."

It didn't surprise me a bit. Fuck progress, I thought.

I slowed down to make a turn to the right, just after a hairpin curve. The rain was driving so hard, I could barely see the road. The highway beneath us felt slick enough to send us into an unintentional skid. I didn't want to die in a car wreck before I had a chance to try out my born-of-desperation plan. I sneaked a look at the clock on the dash. Lukas hardly seemed to notice I'd driven onto narrower and narrower roads. We were dipping down now, into the lower Guadalupe, on Guadalupe River Road, which hugged the river tightly, snaking over it in a few spots. Large ash trees loomed over it, forming a canopy on top that on most days was soft and lovely; right now it, too, was hemming me in, only adding to my fear.

"So you were going to use some under-the-table influence to encourage the county to put pari-mutuel betting up for a referendum? You'd use your lobbyist friend to give it the right kind of publicity, a few dollars at a time. Am I right?"

He nodded his head. "You catch on."

"I try to. Did you even know Mr. Maupin Senior wanted to turn his land over into a trust, to make it an official Civil War site?"

He looked puzzled for once. "Never heard of it, not that I'd give a shit one way or another."

I shook my head. "You're a Vietnam vet, Lukas. You've been to war. Don't you have any feeling for others who've done the same?"

He shook his head violently. "All I see is a bunch of dumb sheep going to the slaughter. I made my experience work for me, even while I was in Southeast Asia. I made money."

"What about Jim? Was he just another dumb sheep, too?"

For the first time, I saw a little crack in Lukas's armor. He didn't say anything for a minute.

"Jim was just a guy from home, when we were about as far from home as either one of us would ever get. You get to know each other fast, that way. What happened later just happened. Everything's not always planned, you know."

"But you'd kill his kid, anyway?"

He dug the revolver into my ribs. Apparently Lukas didn't enjoy trips down memory lane. "I'd do whatever I had to, to survive."

"So killing the kid wouldn't be a big deal," I said. I could feel, all over again, the rage that I'd been suppressing ever since I'd seen that film a few days ago. We'd reached the right spot. "I'm just going to pull off the road here. They're in a cave near here, over toward those trees." I pointed into the distance, toward some cypress trees hugging the banks. I glanced at the clock on the dash one last time. "We might get a little wet, though."

"I can kill you wet or dry," he said, "and the boys too. The old man's just a little extra thrown in for sport." He was quiet for a moment. "No, I take that back. That one's for Jim." He motioned me out of the car.

Well, wet or dry, I wasn't going to die alone if I could take Lukas with me. I opened the door and placed my feet on my beloved hill country ground.

We'd gotten out at the site of one of the oldest Indian settlements in North America, a place where the Tonkawas and the Wacos had camped long before the white man had put his curse on the land. Local historians believed that the area had been occupied by one tribe or another for the last twelve thousand years. I thought of that as I heard the car door shut.

The going would've been funny, if it hadn't been for the probability that this would be my very last walk. Well, hell, I thought, it might as well be memorable. I scurried down some rocks toward the river, Lukas following. That turned out to be the easiest walking we'd be doing. What would've been hard-packed dirt just yesterday had been turned by the rain into pure caliche, the slickest, most slippery substance known to woman or beast. I at least had on running shoes with treads as thick as Michelin tires; Lukas was in some Italian-looking pointy-toed leather shoes that would've been fitting for a good, smooth sidewalk on an extremely clear day. I walked on in front of him, grinning evilly to myself each time I heard him curse his bad footing. I just hoped the gun didn't go off by mistake.

"How far is it?" he grunted. We'd only gone about fifty yards and already the caliche was taking its toll. He'd landed on his butt once but had aimed the gun at me until he got up, full of mud and grime. If he fell down again I'd take a stab at getting the gun.

"Not too much farther," I said. The river, which was normally crystal clear and the color of emerald, was muddy with runoff. I could see that debris was starting to get swept down by what, even without flood conditions, was the strongest hydraulic current on the lower Guadalupe. I was torn between my fears—the killer with a gun on one hand, and nature at her wildest and most terrifying on the other.

Lukas brought me back to the present. "If it's much farther, I'll just kill you here and find the others on my own."

The rain was coming down so hard I began to have trouble seeing clearly. It fell at an angle, driving into my face and my eyes, battering my skin with its ferocity. As we skidded along the riverbank, I tried to visualize the one thing that could save me from sure death. It was one chance in a hundred, nothing that I'd bet on, but it was all I had.

The trees grew closer to the river now, and the footing grew even more treacherous, this time not because of caliche, but because of rocks, mixed in with thick grasses, that could cause you to twist an ankle. My hopes grew even dimmer. I was going to die, alone and horribly, at the hands of a human being who long ago had lost whatever center of light he'd been born with. I thought of my mother and what my death would do to her. I thought of Molly, waiting in vain to hear from me; I thought most of all of Ron, my oldest and best friend, who'd died at the hands of another man cut from Lukas's sorry cloth. I grieved for what I'd be missing myself; I wondered if I'd see Ron on the other side, and if I did, would it even matter anymore? I pictured Littlefield lying on his back while I stroked his stomach, stretching out as far as he could in absolute abandonment and trust.

Just then I lost my footing. I cursed loudly, howling out in a rage at the waste of it all. I tried to get up, but I'd cut my knee on a sharp rock. Blood ran down my leg. Lukas grabbed me by the hair, forcing me to stand.

Just at that moment, I heard the sound I'd been waiting for, a low rumbling that shook the ground. Slumber Falls lay just around the bend, some of the most glorious and dangerous whitewater on the river. Time was running out.

Lukas must've heard it too, because he turned toward the sound with puzzlement written all over his face. As he leaned momentarily away from me, I hit him in the back as hard as I could; I hit him for Jim and his family, for Mr. Maupin, and most of all for those sad, lost women who'd died at his command.

Lukas went down, but he was agile and recovered almost instantly. I grabbed for the gun, which he'd managed to hold onto. As he tried to recover his balance, I kicked him as hard as I could, fear now fueling my strength. He saw the kick coming and grabbed me by the leg, but too late. I'd done some damage. So had he. He twisted and I went down hard on my right side, momentarily out of breath.

The water was louder now, full of fury. In that instant, just for a split second, I thought I could feel my energy connect with that of the river I had rafted with Ron and the guys on hot summer days so long ago. My rage turned into an utter calm that turned out to be far more deadly.

"Let the river decide," I thought. I lunged toward him with all my weight behind the move, catching him in a crouch as he struggled to get to his feet. He went in, backward, astonishment on his face. I thought I heard him cry out in terror, or was that only the sound of the thundering water? I grabbed frantically at some bushes hugging the banks. Too little, too late. I went in after him.

After that, the roaring of the water was all I heard. I'd gone in headfirst, but had ended up on my back somehow, racing down the river feet first, out of all control. Terrified past feeling, I felt the water's power, first sucking me underneath, then allowing me to surface for a moment. I saw myself heading toward huge cypress trees that had grown up in the middle of the river, only to whisk by them, so close I tried to grab hold, so far away there was nothing to hold onto but the water itself. I remember trying to keep my feet together in the water, to avoid the limestone channels that lay just below the surface, wider at the uphill end; more than one unlucky victim had caught a foot in these traps, the force of the water drowning them before they could extricate themselves.

The elements began to batter me for real, throwing me this way and that. I knew I must be close to Slumber Falls, because I could feel the water's quickening pace. The currents were treacherous, whirling me around like the spin cycle on a washing machine, then pulling me down for a long moment before tossing me up for a quick breath that was part water, part air. Suddenly, I heard the loudest sound I'd ever heard, and I knew I was about to go over the falls.

From that moment on, I couldn't tell top from bottom. The water punished me from a thousand different directions. I felt myself hit a boulder, then another. I was pulled underneath headfirst and I struggled wildly, fighting my way to the surface, only to be picked up and tossed back down. My shoulders and rib cage were wrenched one way, my pelvis the other. My lungs burned with a fire previously unknown, and in what consciousness I had left, I knew I was dying at the river's command, one more sacrifice to the gods of the water. I'd asked my question, and now I'd gotten my answer.

At that moment, I slammed into a tree. When I opened my eyes and saw, dimly, what it was, I grabbed on with all the strength I had left. I wrapped my arms and legs around its warm, wet bark. I hugged that old cypress like I'd hugged no lover, no mother, no father, no child, no friend. All the river's raging, all her glory, all her wrath, couldn't make me turn loose of that solid link to life on the only planet I knew.

EPILOGUE

I spent the next five days in an exhausting blur of activity, explaining to the cops, explaining to my clients, and explaining to my friends and family. I'd finally been rescued by the New Braunfels EMS after having been spotted by a curious twelve-year-old, and had spent a night in the hospital, until Lena and Joe came to take me home. Lukas's body had been found on Saturday, caught in what's usually called a strainer—dead logs, fencing, and other debris that lets water, but seldom men, flow through. He'd made it over Slumber Falls, but not much farther.

Lieutenant Jackson put in a good word with the state cops, who finally decided to hear what I'd been saying to them all along. Legally, at least, I was off the hook.

On Sunday afternoon I put Eugene, Jesse, and Greg on a plane to Virginia. Jim and Ruth were ready to get on with their lives, this time without the secrets that had nearly cost them everything they had. They'd invited Eugene to stay with them for a while, and after some hesitation, the old man had agreed to try it. Maybe things would work out for them. I hoped so.

Sunday night found me at Antone's, the home of the blues.

Every R & B or blues musician you ever wanted to see turned up there eventually, and with good reason. Inside those walls, music was the sacred god-king, and anything that wasn't music never made it past the front door. If I'd ever needed this before, I needed it now. Marcia Ball was playing, and it had been way too long since I'd fallen under her magic spell.

She was just as I'd remembered—long and lanky, wearing one of those colorful, loose-fitting hot-weather cotton dresses you see all over Austin. She was a little older, like the rest of us, but looking good. How anyone could play so fast while looking so relaxed had always been a mystery to me. I knocked back a slug of George Dickel and followed it with a swallow of Shiner's.

She still crossed her long legs at the knee when she played the piano and sang, swinging her right leg back and forth to the beat. She went from "That's Enough of That Stuff" straight into the hottest version of "Hot Tamale Baby" I'd ever heard. Her fingers flew over the keys. The crowd went wild, dancing out their frenzy. Marcia's leg swung higher and higher—she was solid cooking, all right, just what the doctor ordered. Her shoe dangled precariously at the ends of her toes, threatening to fly off and away, but it never did.

I took a final sip of my bourbon and signaled for another. Marcia launched into "Love's Spell," a sad R & B ballad, and I closed my eyes. For a moment my throat constricted, and I could see all the hurt and suffering people I had known, and all those I would never see again. The utter sadness of it all washed over me and surrounded me like the thick fog of an August night on the coast of Maine. Then I remembered something I'd heard my mother say all my life, without ever really understanding what she'd meant: "Honey, life's for the living."

She was right.

I opened my eyes and the woman next to me motioned to the dance floor and smiled. "You wanna try it?"

I stood up and held out my hand. "Don't mind if I do," I said.